Bast's
Chosen Ones

& other cat adventures

Dana Bell

WolfSinger Publications   Security, Colorado

Reprints

Chosen One: Full Throttle Space Tales 4 Space Horrors
Taker of Young: Ghost Hunting Critters. "
Characters and concepts from Ghost Hunting Dog/Eye of the
Dog world of J.A. Campbell—used with permission."
The Storm: Frostbitten Fantasies
Danger Said the Dragon: Time Traveling Coffers
The Cat's Creation Tale: All About Eve
Welcome Outcasts: Tales of the Talisman Magazine
& The 2012 Rhysling Anthology
Chandra's Gift: Lorelei Signal ezine
Oasis: Strange Halloween 2012
Shadow: 31 More Nights of Halloween
Bast's Christmas Presents: The Undead that Saved Christmas
Cave Hopes: Of Fur and Fire
Failure: Zombified II
Keeping the Tradition: The Mystical Cat
More Lives: A Flame in the Dark
Darkness in the Heartland: Ultimate Angels

Copyright © 2021 by Dana. Bell

Published by WolfSinger Publications
All rights reserved.

Cover Art copyright 2021 © Lee Ann Barlow

ISBN 978-1-942450-98-6

Table of Contents

Dedication

To God for the inspiration and writing passion.
To Dids, Little One, Tabitha, Sammy and Maximillian
who reside in Heaven's garden.
To Adara and Taj my current fur babies.

Introduction

Since I'm owned by cats, it seems perfectly natural to include them in my stories. They are fun to write and as I've learned, cats do not think like humans. They notice different things and view the world in a way we are unable, at times, to comprehend.

The tales compiled here are a mixture from both published work, and some originals discovered while going through, what seemed to me, my massive computer files.

They are a mixed lot ranging from the distant past, to present day, to the far future. Some are based on real places or events; others are pure imagination or speculation. I've certainly never seen a large cat as an angel, yet they walk in the final piece on this collection.

Most are told from the cat's viewpoint. Some are not. Several are a different alternate take on the same theme. A few are about Bast's Chosen Ones, with a unique take on vampire mythos and cat legends. Not to mention lighthouses, holiday celebrations and more.

So sit back my fellow cat lovers and enjoy these cat tails. Make certain your favorite feline is in your lap. They'll want to read them too.

Chosen One got written because the editor was promised a cat vampire story. The concept took a little time and mixed the mythologies of cats having nine lives and those of ancient Egypt. It's the first of the Cat Vampire series.

Chosen One

My ears twitched slightly as a high-pitched squeak suddenly silenced invaded my hunt and play dreams. I lifted my head from where it rested on my black paws and listened for the sound again. Hearing nothing, I stretched my limber body, being careful not to wake my human companion. She'd had a hard day distributing the few supplies she'd gotten in from the last Earth supply ship. Most of the miners were understanding, but there's always one or two who aren't and they made my human's life a bit more interesting.

I hopped down to the uneven stone floor and up on the narrow ledge of the 'window'. It wasn't really. It's just a hole in the asteroid wall and my human, Leslie is what she calls herself, put up a cloth covered board for me. Sitting down I pushed aside the rough cloth and peered out into the hallway.

A faint stale breeze assaulted my nose smelling of unwashed bodies. Humans are such stinky creatures unlike we felines who instinctively keep ourselves clean. After all, we wouldn't want our rightful prey catching our scent and scampering away.

I blinked my green eyes thankful I could see along the darkened way. No humans were up oddly enough, though there always seemed to be someone about, and the strange silence caught my attention. All I could hear was the usual 'whopf, whopf' of the air and water recycling pumps.

Glancing back, I knew it would be a long while before Leslie was up and about. She'd burrowed deep into her sleeping bag like a serpent in a blast hole. I jumped down and sniffed the outcrop under the window. There was blood, a few bits of skinny tail hair, and an odd scent that seemed both familiar and not. A burning started in my nose and I backed away, using my paw to try and clear the stench away.

I sneezed several times and finally the offensive odor cleared. My back arched and I hissed. A dead one was here. One of the long lifed ones touched with the ancient blessing of Bast. Or maybe it was more of a curse. Among my kind it was spoken of both ways.

Leslie groaned and I looked back up at the window. Maybe I should go back inside and lie beside her. When I did that, she'd settle down. You see, my human came out here after the terrible race and class wars. I don't remember much about them since I was but a youngling and had more important things to think about, like using the zero G litter box correctly and keeping my dignity while floating in the air.

But my human, she lost her entire family in the war. Many living out here in the asteroids had. They'd settled among the twirling rocks to escape the terrible memories and try to scarp out a living by mining the minerals and precious stones, like the flashy politicians back on Earth said they could. Not that many have hit it rich. Most make just enough to pay the taxes on their claims and buy a few supplies.

My head popped up as a leathery sound snaked over the rock. The tunnel serpents were dangerous and deadly. They weren't native but an odd variation contrived by some gene expert to keep down the population of the skinny tails. Not that it had worked. Instead, the creatures had escaped and liked to den close to the humans, sending many of our companions to the final sleep. And so, we felines hunt them and send the serpents to a swift and final end.

Well, as quick of an end as we allowed. What fun is food if we don't get to play with it first?

I scrunched down and began to track the noise, rubbing my side against the smooth rock, trying to be silent as I slowly stalked my prey. Around a corner, the red, white, black and aqua snake coiled, its velvet tongue lashing out at another of my kind.

No, not my kind, I corrected myself as the rotting stench touched my sensitive brown nose. I sneezed and jumped back just as the serpent swung toward me and struck. I heard its head rattle against the unstable boulder barely missing me.

The stinking mass pounced, sinking deep canine like fangs into the scaly flesh. I watched in horror as the long body flopped, causing pebbles to skitter scatter over the floor. Finally, the snake stilled, its tongue slithering out of its mouth, a few green drops of its venom splattering on the stone.

"It's dead," the other told me. "You should take more care."

"You shouldn't be here," I hissed back. My body trembled. Though I had heard the stories, none had prepared me for the true appearance of the creature. Short cropped tan fur scattered with black spots, towering above me by at least a full head, ebony claws extended making an 'erch' noise as it moved.

It lifted a giant paw and casually licked the serpent blood mixed with green venom away. When the necessary washing was done, it stared at me with round yellow-red eyes.

"I am nothing to fear."

"You're so…big." I could think of nothing else to say.

"We are the first ones. Not contaminated by the touch of humans."

It sounded almost condescending. As if by choosing to companion with Leslie, I was less than it was.

"I saved your life this night. Remember my favor well." It bounded away and I stood staring after it. How could a feline so large, be gone so quick?

~ * ~

When morning came, I wondered if I had indeed, encountered one of the favored ones of Bast. I awakened as was usual, lying beside my human. She smiled at me and rubbed behind my ear. My eyes half closed and I purred for her. Leslie fed me my breakfast of dried sea dweller and I lapped my water to rid myself of the salty tang.

As was normal, she went to the trading post to haggle with the few stragglers who would come in today to see if there was anything left. I think she said she had a case of unmarked soup, several boxes of crackers, and a package of cookies she was saving special for someone.

I again sat in the window watching the humans hurry by. Not that I cared what they did with their day. I just enjoyed the few who stopped to give me a friendly pet and sometimes sneak a treat they'd secreted in their pockets.

Old George always brought me a green sharp scented treat I loved to roll in. I heard him say he grew it for all the cats (I really don't like that word) and he felt we deserved it for all the de-rodent work we did. Most of the humans just rolled their eyes, but he'd wink at me like he knew I understood.

Of course, several of us lived with him, so I suspect he knows we do.

He came by as was normal and pulled the cotton bag out of his pocket. I saw something hanging out of his other pocket and batted at it. When he turned, I flattened my ears against my head.

"Just a dead snake," he reassured me, taking some of the scented stuff on his fingers and running them over my fur. "Found it down the hallway there. Quite peculiar." He shrugged. "See ya later, Blackie." He trotted away.

Blackie. He always called me that. Leslie called me Shadow. My true name is, no, I mustn't even think it. The ancient one might hear, or so the legends say, and then have power over me. I can't allow that.

I lost part of my day in a haze of pungent leafy enjoyment and took my normal nap on my human's bed. Upon waking I bathed myself yet again, no self-respecting feline is ever dirty, ate a few bits of the dry stuff Leslie left for me, drank more water and prepared to go off exploring again.

Quickly I checked the small room for any unwelcome guests. Finding none, I padded out and down the rock hewn hallway. I had to dodge uncaring human feet several times. Many don't watch out for us and I don't remember how many times my tail or paws have been stepped on. They don't even apologize and that is truly offensive.

Finally, I got to the trading post.

Old George was there and he had the snake spread out on the old board counter. Leslie was sitting on a barrel watching. I jumped up and batted at the dead serpent.

"Shadow, be careful!" Leslie warned as she tried to move me away from it.

"It's quite dead," George said. "Though, I don't think any of the cats killed it."

I wish he'd stop calling us cats.

"Why do you say that?"

"Normally, when a cat kills one, the neck is broken and it's partially eaten." He turned the intact snake over. "This one has a wound on it and when I tried to give it to Bossy,"

Bossy lives here in the post. She's the oldest of us and tells us stories about Earth. It's from her I heard about the ancient ones.

"She only hissed and tried to scratch me."

"Shadow doesn't seem to be afraid of it."

"He ain't claiming it neither." George scratched his shaggy dirty hair and grimaced. Maybe he'd figured out he was dirty and needed to bathe. "Strange."

"I just hope it doesn't mean we have yet another pest to deal with." Leslie shook her head. "I'm getting tired of us figuring out how to fight one problem only to have another crop up."

"It's called life, my dear girl."

"If you say so." She quickly ran a hand over my back. "What do you need, George?"

I ignored them as they discussed what he needed, what Leslie actually had, and all the details of the transaction they finally agreed upon. Old George put the serpent back in his pocket and ambled away.

~ * ~

Over the next few cycles, several tunnel serpents and skinny tails were found all over the asteroid. The other felines avoided the kill spots, but I found myself drawn to them, sniffing the odd scents and sneezing out the sharp hurt until I no longer needed to.

I'd told the others about my encounter with the ancient one. Bossy had stared at me with her one good eye. The other she'd lost in a fight with a skinny tail.

"You've been chosen," she'd told me.

"Chosen?" I hadn't understood.

"The stories say," she'd continued, "the ancient ones select one of us."

"For what?"

"I do not know. A chosen one has never come back and told us."

Quite honestly, I didn't know whether to be concerned or not. So, I continued my days of sleeping, eating, bathing, hunting, being pet and receiving treats from the humans. What else is there in the life a feline?

Perhaps I should have paid more attention to Bossy's warning. Or perhaps, I should have known there was little to fear.

For when it happened, I had been hunting under the many metal moving parts of the air pump station. The skinny tails seem to like it in here. There're so many places they can hide and we felines have a hard time catching them when they dart into the narrow places we cannot squeeze our flexible bodies into.

I had cornered a skinny tail and made ready to pounce, only to feel a sharp pain in my head. I shook it and my vision blurred as drops of heavy red fell over my muzzle. The tang of hot blood touched my tongue and I sensed it was my own.

The skinny tail wiggled toward me its beady black eyes keenly watching. Its sharp little teeth plunged into my paw and I yowled in torment. I tried to swipe at it and break its neck, but my paw would not obey. Heavily I fell, my head smacking into something hard. I heard a 'kkk' and knew I would not rise nor be able to stop the nipping teeth tearing at my body.

That was the last I remembered.

When I awoke again, I found myself lying on a soft bed. I heard the 'sprrrr, sprrr' of water nearby and I suddenly found I longed for a drink. Shakily I got up, surprised to find my body intact and not in pain.

I blinked, raising my head to gaze around. Above a gauzy fabric waved in the wind attached to marble columns covered in bright colorful designs. All around I could smell the delightful pungent tang of my favorite green plant. Surrounding my furred bed was a soft, fine powder I had never seen before.

Carefully I extended my paw and touched the powder, quickly withdrawing it when the substance spread under my touch. I wasn't sure I liked it, but I was so thirsty.

The powder was soft under my paws and though not easy to walk upon, it did not impede me to my destination. I lowered my head to lap at the clear water, feeling the liquid revive me in a way I could not express.

"So you've awakened, warrior."

I had not heard the female approach. I jumped back and whirled to face her; my black hair puffed up along my spine.

"You're in no danger here." She sat down and blinked her green-yellow eyes at me, her bushy spotted tail draped over her paws.

She looked like the ancient one. She had the same tan fur and black spots, but she wasn't as large as he had been.

"You are welcome in my temple."

"Your temple?"

A deep amused purr rumbled from her chest. It was then I noticed the odd gold circle about her neck.

"I am Bast, warrior."

Bast! I pushed my belly onto the powder and lowered my head. I must pay proper respect to the goddess.

"You died in honor, warrior. There is no need to crawl upon the sand as would an adder."

She rose. "Come. There is a matter yet to be resolved."

I got to my paws. The sand clung to my belly. I'd have to clean it off later. I followed Bast beyond the place where I had awakened to an open dwelling of many smooth stairs and golden columns. Standing on each side where humans in thin clothing, their heads bald and odd markings on their faces.

"My priests who have chosen to serve me in the afterlife," she explained.

At the top I stopped. Bast strolled to pile of fur and took her place. All around her were other felines. A mass of browns, blacks, whites, and so many other colors, I could not sort them in my mind.

Bast's head turned and the ancient one I had encountered joined us. My heart began to pound as if I had hunted well and now was the time of play.

"So, he has passed beyond," the ancient one said.

"He has," Bast agreed. "Yet, the debt has not been repaid."

"It has not." His yellow-red eyes looked at me. "Unfortunate."

"Perhaps not. Warrior," Bast summoned.

I dared to approach her.

"You owe a debt to this my favored one. Would you choose to repay? Or do you intend to dwell here with me?"

"I have already passed beyond." I did not understand the choice offered.

Again her chest echoed the purring laugh. "Humans have legends of us."

I still did not understand.

"My offer stands."

"I can release him," the ancient one offered.

"No. This one has always had great promise."

"And if it was my wish to repay?" I almost feared her answer. I thought she would return me to my damaged and tortured body.

"That was burned by your human."

"So how?" I did not understand how such a thing was possible nor how she'd known my thought.

"I bestow my favor on many." Her tongue darted out and touched the muzzle of the ancient one. "Besides, humans need to be reminded of their proper place. And ours as well."

"And that is?" I still didn't truly understand.

"We were worshipped once, warrior. So we should be again. Now, is it truly your wish to repay, warrior?"

"It is."

"So be it." Bast came to me and stole my breath.

~ * ~

"Sure looks like Blackie," Old George said as he rubbed my head. I nipped at his fingers. He had my favorite leafy smell on them.

"Well, we both know that's not possible." Leslie scratched behind my ear and turned away to shelf the new shipment of supplies.

"Poor ole boy."

I saw Leslie wipe liquid from under her eye. "Well, at least you didn't see the body." She shuddered. "It was horrible."

"Smart thing you did burning it."

"It was the best thing."

"Where'd you find this fella?" His hand ran the length of my back.

"Captain of the supply ship found him in the hold. Knew I'd lost mine and offered him to me."

"Smart man."

"Guess so." She sighed. "I miss Shadow."

I jumped down bored with the conversation. It was time to hunt and I had in my mind to find the skinny tail who had ended my first life. Bast had promised me my revenge and the goddess always kept her word.

Padding out on the familiar stone, I was joined by the ancient one. The other felines saw us coming and darted into hiding spots until they passed. They knew we were no longer like them.

"I found the skinny tail," the ancient one told me.

"Good. I want to play with it for a long time before I kill it."

"As is proper."

"So, I have another debt to repay."

"You will have a long time to do so. And I am patient, young-ling."

I knew his words to be true. For as Bast told me, humans have many legends of us and the one they scoff at even as they speak it, is truth. We do indeed have nine lives and I have another eight to repay the ancient one before I return to Bast and her temple.

I just didn't know that I'd live them as a chosen one—as a vampire.

This story is the sequel to Chosen One. Not only is Taker of Young one of the Cat Vampire series, but also the first of the Dollhouse Stories. The homes and their descriptions are based on two, Sea House and Great Aunt's Victorian. The setting is borrowed from a Colorado ghost town. It has also appeared in an anthology full of animals who hunt ghosts, vamps, and other critters.

Taker of Young

Bells echoed over the water, reaching my ears and causing them to twitch. I found the reflex annoying. I raised one paw and listened intently. A foghorn bellowed, breeching the thick mist shrouding the town. Rancid scents of dead fish invaded my nose and I wanted to retch. I preferred my swimmers live, their cool blood a soothing liquid to quench my thirst.

Daring to move forward, I examined what little I knew of the small town. It had once made its living by the riches of gold, silver, ores, saloons and brothels. The mine flooded as the waters rose, engulfing three sides of the bluff.

When this had happened, none knew. From what I could see, the main street supported a grocery, a doctor's office, a vet clinic, and a few other assorted stores. Farther out near the water's edge stood a sprawling school, the windows dark for the holidays. On the farthest point sat a light house, its beam piercing the thick damp fog.

Higher on the ridge, their colorful sparkling lights joyful around windows and roof lines, were the houses of those who lived here. Great trees bent to the will of heavy snow and ice covered the ground and barren bushes.

"This way."

I turned my head to gaze at my long-time companion Seti. His bronze, black spotted fur blended into the building's shadow, keeping him invisible to weak human eyes.

"Where must we go?" I doubted I could be seen at all. My short black fur helped me hide.

"The blue and white marble house." He padded over to me; his head upturned. "There."

Since he pointed it out, I could see it. It didn't stand on the highest point like the Victorian house. The blue marble home sat nearest the ocean's edge.

Seti must have noticed my interest in the Victorian. "The Guardian and her Protector live overlooking the village."

"Who are they?"

"The Guardian has, since this colony was founded, been the one who kept evil from invading and destroying both the town and its people. The Protector is unknown to her, yet keeps any dark presence from her entering her home."

"Why are we going to another home?" It would make more sense to go to the one who needed our help directly.

"That is not where Bast has instructed us to go. You should well know by now; we were made to be her warriors. To protect those who have destinies she wishes to see fulfilled. "

Of course I did. I just didn't always understand her methods.

Seti took the lead, trotting up the icy dirt road lined with red and green lights, like the lamp posts I'd seen on history discs, which humans had used during the late Nineteenth Century. As I remembered, then, they'd been filled with gas. I wondered what power source the colonists used.

Dampness invaded my fur. While it didn't chill me, it annoyed instead. I still didn't like getting wet, as most cats don't, despite having been changed by the goddess. Seti and I were Chosen Ones, or a form of vampire, but very unlike the few human ones I'd encountered.

Once we reached the teal door, Seti jumped up the two steps and meowed loudly, his thick tail slowly moving back and forth.

Footsteps came from behind the door, a human coming to answer our plea.

Brightness as she opened the door, causing my night adjusted eyes to blink. Her red hair was haloed in the light from what must be the main room. She wore a long blue dress, decorated in a seashell pattern. I sniffed, blinking my yellow eyes in surprise. The woman who stood there was not human, rather one who walked the night. Oddly her scent filled my nose with spring wildflowers. Hers was not the normal mix of decay and blood I had become familiar with.

"She is of Bast," Seti explained, as the woman moved back to allow us entrance.

The room felt warm and pleasant. A fire crackled and I moved to the fireplace and allowed the flames to dry my fur. Several other Chosen Ones were draped over the blue flower print couch and chairs. A couple sat in the window, their heads barely visible among the flowers.

"Welcome," the woman greeted. "You are Seti." She bowed her head. I noticed her pale skin and blue eyes. "You are called Blackie."

I had actually never chosen a name. Most humans tended to call me Blackie, so I just accepted it. I urped in response.

Shuddering wind moaned past the window. A gray kitten jumped out and dashed under the chair. Its smell told me it was not a Chosen One. I wondered why it lived here. Most cats avoided us.

"The rest of its litter is here, in various homes." Seti pulled at his claws. "That is part of why we are here."

I'd grown used to going where Bast sent us. I had not yet had the opportunity to pay my debt to Seti after he saved my mortal life from a poisonous snake. I found I liked his company, and he mine. Often Chosen Ones became solitary. That seemed to be changing as mankind expanded beyond their mother world and settled new ones.

"There is fresh fish in the kitchen." The woman sat slowly down. Several cats scattered to make room for her. "I am Gennie."

Seti headed to the open door. I followed taking in the sea theme throughout both rooms. Yellow walls and appliances warmed the kitchen. A bright blue hutch sat against the wall with a matching table. Both had painted orange starfish on them.

Below the large window fish swam in a bowl. Seti caught one, and drained it. I did the same. Sated, I returned to stand at the door, gazing at the woman. The kitten had curled into her lap, its eyes half closed in pleasure, its purr loud.

"The kitten has a destiny." Seti washed his face. "We are here to save it, its siblings and," He blinked. "Other young."

"Who would harm a kitten?"

"This town has a dark presence that haunts it. The Guardian, in the Victorian home, has long tried to keep it safe."

"Not successfully."

"She has, until recently."

The horn again blared, the walls shaking slightly. High pitched scratches raked the kitchen window and I whirled, hissing at the intrusion. I heard my warning echoed from the other Chosen Ones.

"It grows worse." Gennie rose, placing the kitten on the couch. She went up the stairs and I barely heard her footsteps as she crossed the floor above us. A chill air crept back down. Excited yips and clicking nails echoed down and two collies trotted behind the woman as she descended the stairs.

Well, one grown white breasted, long haired brown collie, with a pup of the same coloring. Instead of rushing over to us, they sat beside the couch, although their tails wagged endlessly.

Gennie lightly rested her hand on the dog's head. "This is Sheba and her only surviving pup Shag."

A chill swept through my body. While Gennie had not said it, yet, Seti had. I fully understood the dark presence was taking more than just kittens. Pups were at stake as well. I wondered if this only affected us, or did it take human babies as well?

Seti answered my unasked question. "The Guardian has managed to protect them."

It would be up to us to protect the kittens and pups. I yowled loudly and my body quivered.

Let the hunt begin.

~ * ~

"Where are we going?" I asked as Seti and I climbed the icy road.

"I need to speak with the Protector."

"I thought the Guardian lives here. Should we not speak with her?" My eyes took in the purple Victorian with the blue trim.

"If it were possible." Seti climbed the stairs. "It's best to speak to her Protector."

Seti had already explained why the Guardian had a Protector. I didn't see why we needed to talk to it.

Seti quietly crossed the porch and sat down beside a gray stone gargoyle with a bright red Santa hat on its head. "Hello."

"I look ridiculous, don't I?" a gravelly voice replied. Slowly the gargoyle turned its head. "I wear it to make her happy."

"As a Protector should."

"How may I serve you Chosen One of Bast?"

"How fares the Guardian?"

"She is young. Learning slowly what took her Great Aunt decades to master. She does not hear or know the many magics."

"She was not taught?" Blackie heard the surprise in Seti's tone.

"There was not time." The gargoyle slowly rose, stretching each of its stone legs. "She came from off world months after her Great Aunt passed." The hat slipped slightly. "She has found the doll house village."

"That is good."

I had no idea what that meant and waited to see if I'd be enlightened.

Seti sat down. A good sign because it meant he had something to share. "I lived here when it was built. The first Guardian lived in a log cabin with her husband and two children. He built it for their daughter so her mother could teach," he paused. "I do not remember the girl's name."

"Teach her what," I prompted.

"How to protect the town." He rose. "The dark one discovered its purpose and caused a fire that would have killed them all, had the dogs and cats living there not alerted their people to the danger."

My companion stared at the door. "The village slipped into another dimension."

"Only appearing," the Protector added, "when needed."

A type of magic then perhaps mixed with science, often difficult to separate the two as I had learned through the centuries.

"We are here," Seti informed the Protector, "to save the other young."

The Protector turned its thick neck toward the door, the stained glass reflecting the colorful lights surrounding the frame. "You will need to access the little village. I don't know how you will. It's in the attic and may not be there for you to see."

Seti sniffed. "There are cats here."

The gargoyle smiled. "She has a soft heart." It settled back into its position, once again seeming to be nothing but stone, the hat still on its head.

"Come." Seti perched outside the door and yowled pitifully.

I added my cry to his.

There were steps on the other side of the door and it swung open. A young woman appeared, wrapped in a heavy fluffy house-coat, her dark hair barely visible. "You poor things." She stepped back. "Well, come in."

Playing the part, we both hesitantly entered, our heads darting each direction as if afraid of attack. I could smell the cats and dogs. Somewhere too, a large bird lived.

"This way." We followed her through the house, up two flights of carpeted stairs to the upmost floor. Light flickered in the window. A white wicker lounge sat in the turreted area and several kittens peered down at us, their yellow eyes glittering.

"Food is over there." She pointed toward the back of the house. "I suspect you'll find it on your own." She went back downstairs.

I glanced around. The room had been painted gray. On one wall angels, each in a different pose, perched overlooking the stairs. The rest of the room was dedicated to the ancient art of sewing.

"Is this the attic?" I looked at Seti.

"No." His gaze drifted upwards. He stopped near the back of the room, his eyes resting on a trap door I had not seen. "We need to go up there."

While we are excellent climbers, going up the narrow ladder attached to the wall would be difficult, if not impossible. We certainly couldn't unlock the latch.

Seti's tail twitched. "Since we can't communicate with the guardian, we will need the Protectors help."

~ * ~

Dark had fallen upon the house. Outside branches clawed the windows, the loud scraping noise frightening the kittens who abandoned their warm huddle on the settee. They crouched underneath, shivering.

Seti sat beneath the attic trap door, cocking his head side to side, as if he listened for rodent scuttles and squeaks.

I remembered their warm filling blood.

A creak on the stairs diverted my attention. My eyes saw a shadowy figure creeping around and across the floor. I started to arch my back and hiss a warning, when I realized it had no smell. This was no dark presence, nor a living creature.

"I would ask how you got into the house," Seti said, turning his head. "But I suspect you have done this many times."

"Many," the Protector agreed. "You need to go up there." He

pointed a stone finger at the bolted trap door.

"Fortunate you are more humanoid than animal shaped," Seti said. "You have hands to assist us."

The Protector had pointed ears, and its stone hair, what I could see beneath the hat, seemed wavy. Its gray stone face didn't look human. More like a mythic creature from days long past.

Making no noise despite its heavy stone, the Protector scurried up the wall ladder and undid the bolt. He came back down, then carried first Seti, then myself, up and set us upon the dusty attic floor. I could see faint human footprints, no doubt belonging to the Guardian.

"I must return to my perch. You must have the guardian open the door for you."

"Do as you must," Seti replied.

My thin tail slowly waved back and forth, the mustiness tickling my nose. All around boxes and furniture leaned against the walls. Wrapping paper lay stacked near the only round window, where the faint twin moons peeked inside.

Seti sat down. "We must wait."

"For what?"

"The tiny village. It's not here."

The Protector had warned us it might not be. I did not understand how it could appear. The space seemed too small.

I had seen tiny villages before, often in forgotten museums. They took up entire, huge rooms.

"How can it appear? There is no space for it." Understanding magic is something I still haven't mastered.

"It is the magic of the place."

"Our wait could be long." I licked a spot on my shoulder.

"Perhaps," Seti agreed.

"How will its appearing help us?"

"As I remember," Seti jumped up and settled on top of box. "Each home reflects the actions of those who live there, including animals. We should be able to hunt the evil easily, instead of searching the entire town."

A mouse or scamperer, as I prefer to call them, ducked out of a box and twitched its nose at us before disappearing into a crack.

"At least we will not starve," Seti observed.

~ * ~

Nights here are longer than most other worlds. I gazed out the window and watched the humans below. The Guardian spoke with her neighbor, a woman with blond hair and fair skin. Around them frolicked several dogs that probably belonged to them, a long black-haired Dachshund, a Scottie dog the same color, and an Irish Setter with her pup.

I watched intently, trying to detect if an arm of darkness reached out for the youngling.

"They are safe with the Guardian." My companion had joined me. "They have adapted well to their world." He licked his paw. "They have two sleeps, going to bed when night falls, rising in the early morning when they go to visit friends, then return to their beds until the sun rises."

After a time, the door below opened and the guardian returned with the Irish Setters and the Scottie.

"What if the Guardian discovers the attic door is open and closes it?"

"Bast will provide."

Of course. Seti always gave me the same reply when I asked a question he did not wish to answer. Not that we had much to fear if we became trapped. We had food and dark places to seek shelter from the sun.

I felt a rustling of my fur like human fingers stroked my back. I whirled to see who had come and blinked at the sight before me. Tiny houses with sparkling lights, sitting as they did in the village. Even the lighthouse sat in its place of honor.

Bells sounded yet again, wrapping the attic space in their sound.

Seti padded over the village, gazing in the windows, sniffing, as he does when he hunts.

I had been with Seti long enough to know there are times when I needed to wait on him and do as he instructed. My eyes watched for movement, for any hint of the presence we sought.

There!

I hissed. Seti lifted his head. Slowly I stalked my prey, my body low on the floor. Seti matched my movements, coming around the edge of the miniature village. Both of us paused, watching the black blob attempting to ooze through the barn doors where animals in their stalls slept and several young humans in the loft. A doll turned and I could see the tiny chest moving.

So. The tiny town reflects what is happening in the real village. An interesting magic I had never seen before.

"It's after the chicks!" I could see them tucked under their mother's feathers. I wondered how none there could sense the danger.

"We must stop it." Seti put out his paw setting it firmly on the black. I heard a squeal. "Good. We can catch it."

It rolled away from the door and headed for the Victorian dollhouse. We watched as it ascended the hill, stopping at the bottom of the stairs. The Protector sat on the porch, the Santa hat slightly askew.

"It cannot get into the house!" Seti slunk around the tiny town, crouching just inches away and pounced on the blob. It squiggled in his paws.

"How do we stop it?" If it had been rightful prey, we could drain it like a mouse or a fish.

I heard barking. I ran to the window to look out. Sheba ran up the road. How had she gotten out of Gennie' house? The Collie jumped on the shadow. It pushed her back and she landed with a faint thud on the ground. Immediately she leapt to her feet and attacked again.

"How do we weaken it?" I asked.

"I am not sure." Seti griped the blob even harder with his claws. Below a high-pitched wail filled the air. I heard the kittens yowl, the dogs howl, and the bird screech.

I blinked. The Protector hovered outside the window, the hat still on his head.

"The Protector does not fight?" I asked.

"Guards the door only." Seti struggled with the blob. It oozed between his claws almost escaping as it struggled to get to the door, now unprotected.

"Get back to your post!" I ordered the Protector. "Keep it out!" I dashed back to the miniature house to see what happened.

Darting down, the Protector took up its post again. The blob shivered and Sheba attacked, biting the blackness.

I began to hear waves. Where there had been rough flooring,

water rippled, mimicking the real town surrounded by water on three sides.

The blob struggled harder, trying to escape. Perhaps it feared the water.

"Can it drown?" I inquired.

"I do not know." Seti began to pull it toward the lighthouse cliff. The tiny doll house dog representing Sheba raced after it.

Seti yanked and pulled, edging closer and closer to the steep edge. I circled around to the lighthouse, standing on the edge, the water so close I could feel and smell its fishy dampness. I wanted to make certain that if our prey escaped, I would be there to catch it.

Seti backed across the floor, dragging the blob as it pulsated and squirmed to escape. He managed to wiggle around, his front claws extended over the cliff's edge. Retracting his claws, he released his prey.

The blob didn't immediately fall. It reached up a black tentacle and wrapped around one brown paw, tugged hard, trying to pull Seti with it.

My companion dug in his other claws, trying to pull back. Seti's hind legs slipped, since nothing was there for him to grip. The momentum thrust him forward toward the cliff edge and the water below.

I jumped, grabbing the blob, my claws ripping its body. I heard it scream as it fell.

My body tumbled through darkness. I could see Seti's head above me, staring down. The next thing I knew, I hit cold water and dropped deeply beneath the waves. I struggled in whirling wet, trying to escape. Not that I would drown. My body would go into a deep sleep until I washed up on shore somewhere. Not that I wanted that to happen.

I pushed hard, hoping to reach the surface. My head pushed through and I wildly looked around trying to figure out where the shore might be. The two moons provided some light, but not enough to help.

A flash of white danced across the waves. I blinked, trying to understand where it came from. There was another and another.

The lighthouse beacon!

I could see the round structure perched on the cliff's edge. I started swimming toward it.

Waves rocked me constantly, trying to pull me further away. I pushed on, hoping I would not be lost in the vast ocean of this world.

Teeth grabbed my neck. I wanted to fight, but my body instinctively went limp. I feared perhaps some predator had claimed me. Granted, I would not die in their belly, but it would be very unpleasant until it spat me out.

I don't know how long it took to reach the shore. The teeth dropped me.

"Good girl, Sheba." A warm towel surrounded my soaked fur. "Easy, Blackie. You're safe." I recognized Gennie's voice.

"Seti?" I panted.

"At my home." Lotus blossoms filled my nose. I rested against the woman as she carried me up the narrow cliff trail and to her home. She placed me before the fire and I let the warmth dry my fur. I was too tired to do it myself.

Seti came to me, giving my head an affectionate lick.

"How did you get out of the attic?" I asked.

"When I realized there were portals, I went to Gennie and asked for her help."

I turned my head to where Gennie rubbed Sheba with a thick blanket. She scratched behind dog's head ear. "Sheba was already in the water searching for you when I arrived. I waited until you were both safe."

"Thank you, Gennie. Bast did well when she chose you."

"Thank you and you're welcome, Blackie." She reached for another blanket and wrapped it around Sheba, having the collie lay down before the fireplace. "You have rid us of the darkness that has claimed too many lives. It is we who owe you."

"Bast sends us where we're needed," Seti reminded her.

"And you have earned a rest. You are welcome to stay in my home until the goddess needs you."

"Thank you." Seti turned his attention to me. "It seems you have paid back your debt to me. It meant to destroy me."

Sun light began to creep into the house. Gennie rose and dropped the drapes. "There are many places to sleep. Blackie, I hope you don't mind sharing the fire with Sheba."

"I would be honored."

Sheba wagged her tail.

"I will the sleep the day and in the night, you can give me an answer, Seti and Blackie." Gennie gave Sheba a quick pat on the head.

"We will stay," Seti assured her. "We must make certain the darkness is gone and that all young are safe."

"As it should be." She hurried up the stairs. The kittens of the house scurried after her.

"So," I said, "we are to stay together."

"Unless you are tired of my company."

"I am not." I moved so I could snuggle against Sheba. She put her head down on her paws, her tail thumping the floor. Her pup bounced in and settled next to her.

"They are not ordinary dogs, are they?" I asked Seti.

"They are not." He stretched beside us, one paw touching mine. "They have a long history. Perhaps, tonight, I will tell you."

"I would like that." I rested against Sheba and allowed her breathing to soothe me to sleep.

Lighthouses have a long-honored history and often a ghostly one. Our Long Lost is the first of two tales set on one, but not on a familiar shore. Instead, it sits in the depths of space.

Our Long Lost

Cali the cat had vanished. Peter sighed and gazed around the storage hold. The feline's trick was pretty impressive considering how few places existed to hide in the lighthouse.

"Want some help, Dad?"

With a glance at his tall teen-age son, he nodded. "Where's Maisy?" Since his thirteen-year-old daughter had pitched a hysterical fit over her cat's disappearance, it still amazed him she hadn't volunteered to help search for it.

"Shut up in her room crying."

Not for the first time Peter wished his wife was still alive. No doubt she would have known how to console their daughter. Unfortunately, her exploratory ship, the *Teresa Spencer*, had vanished somewhere in Orion's Belt. The Space Service had declared them missing, presumed lost with all souls aboard, after all the normal delayed mission reports ceased.

Peter straightened his shoulders. He needed to be strong for his children. "Let's get to it."

For the next couple of hours, they moved every heavy container, many filled with food and other supplies they'd need for Peter's three-year assignment. It was a prime pick and he'd been lucky to get it. Plus the Service had bent regulations, given the circumstances, and allowed him to bring his two children.

"The cat's just not here, Dad." Josh rubbed his dirty hands on his retro blue jeans. "And Cali was still here after the *Amber Spice* left."

"I know." Peter shivered. Seconds ago he'd been hot and sweaty replaced by a shivering cold creeping along his spine. A flickering shadow oozed into a corner. He blinked his tired eye convinces they played tricks on him.

Things would have been simpler if Cali had stowed away on the passing inbound ship. The captain would have dropped the animal at the Io base and the first official colonization vessel out would have brought Cali home. Felines were valuable. They kept rodents in check.

"So now what?" His son leaned against one of the tall round containers labeled flash frozen chicken.

"We keep looking." Not much else they could do. "Come on. I think we've both earned a cup of hot chocolate."

Josh grinned and followed Peter as they went back up the metal stairs. He slid the hatch closed, hoping he hadn't inadvertently sealed the cat below. There had been many times Cali had vanished at their Martian home only to turn up in some obviously overlooked spot, like a laundry basket full of clean clothes. He couldn't remember how many times he'd cleaned white fur off his dark gray uniforms.

Out of habit he glanced at the huge com screen dominating one wall. The dull screen contained no waiting messages. He knew very few ships were due to pass for the next six weeks, unless one of the deep space probes returned unexpectedly. Their arrivals and discoveries caused great excitement in the service and the news channels back home.

He continued on to the living area. The décor was a soft blue with matching furniture, a tiny dinette set and a functional kitchenette. He poured water into two mugs and placed them in the zap waiting a few minutes before removing the steaming cups.

He glanced at his son. Josh has sprawled out on the couch, a comic book somehow appearing from nowhere. Peter hadn't seen it before. "Where'd you get that?"

"Traded with one of the cargo handlers." Josh turned the page.

At least Josh was reading so Peter let it slide. It wasn't an uncommon practice to trade books, comics or other things with passing ships. He wondered how many others had read the same, how many hands it had passed from and who would trade for it next.

"Any good?" He poured the dry cocoa contents into the mugs and stirred them. If he remembered correctly there should be a package of marshmallows. He rummaged around the compact pantry until he found them. He tossed a few in each cup and put them on the table. "It's ready."

Josh got up, comic in hand, and joined his father. His son sipped the hot cocoa as he kept reading.

"What's the story about?"

Not taking his eyes from the page Josh answered. "Some weird guy in a metal suit battling baddies."

"Pretty much the same theme in all of them, isn't it?" Peter savored the sweet cocoa taste and shivered again. Later, he'd check the heating system.

"Yeah, but it's fun." Josh took another swig. "I think this is a really old one since I don't remember seeing it in the comic stores back home."

"Worth the trade then."

"Always is."

"Is that hot chocolate I smell?"

Peter looked up at his daughter. She'd dressed in a much too tight red top with a pink tutu skirt. Rainbow colored jewelry completed her ensemble along with knee length fringed black boots. Her hair fell in dark strands around her oval face reminding him of his wife.

He didn't like Maisy's fashion sense and hoped three years on the lighthouse would break both her taste for it and her ties with friends who tended to get her into trouble at school and the other places in the dome.

"Want some?" Peter rose to make it.

"I can *do* it." She flounced past her father. Josh rolled his brown eyes.

Sitting back down, Peter took another drink. His daughter busied herself making the hot treat before gingerly joining them at the table. "Find my cat?"

"Not yet."

She sniffed dramatically and buried her sorrow in the hot chocolate, the top brimming with marshmallows.

"Better take it easy on those, little sis," Josh teased. "Not like we can dash out and buy more any time we want."

"Oh, shut up!" Her mug landed a little too hard on the white surface, and a few precious drops of chocolate splashed over. "If I'd been left at Aunt Martha's like I'd asked–"

"I thought we'd cleared that all up," Peter interrupted. "Your

Aunt Martha is about to ship out on the *Corey Slide*."

"Yeah, in a year and a half!"

Josh turned a page and added, "And she'd be gone most of the time training." He temporarily stopped reading to glare at his sister. "No time to look after a bratty kid."

"I'm not a brat!" She stuck her tongue out at her brother.

"Enough! Both of you!" Peter was used to their fighting, but after looking for the cat all day instead of cleaning the lenses like he needed to, he didn't have the patience for it. "You're both on your own for dinner."

"Fine by me," Maisy grabbed her partially empty cup and vanished upstairs to her bedroom. If she could have slammed her door, Peter suspected he would have heard a loud bang.

"I'll make sure she eats more than just peanut butter, chocolate and popcorn," her brother promised.

Peter shook his head. "If that's what she wants for dinner, that's okay."

"Feel bad we didn't find Cali?"

His son knew him maybe a bit too well. "A little. Do me a favor and check the food recycler." The pesky rats liked the area and it was the one place they hadn't looked. "Maybe Cali is hunting."

Josh wrinkled his nose, reminding him again of his wife who had a habit of doing that, before returning his attention to the comic.

Peter climbed the steep stairs up to the light. In a cupboard he removed the supplies he needed and went to work cleansing and polishing the lenses.

Funny how some technology advanced, yet the simplicity of the lighthouse refractors stayed. The electronic beams caused 'pings', like the ancient sonar, allowing navigators to know their correct position in space.

Not that Peter's assigned lighthouse sat in deep space. Its position was just beyond the planetoid Pluto, but not reaching into the meteor and asteroid filled ort cloud sea.

He stretched when he finished before returning below. The scent of peanut butter, popcorn and chocolate filled his nose. He grinned, hoping Maisy enjoyed her dinner.

He made himself a light supper of soup and a cheese sandwich. Quiet met his ears and he figured both his children were either sleeping or engaged in some favorite activity. Josh would be reading. Maisy no doubt would be moping, both from her forced separation from her so called 'friends' and that Houdini cat.

The thought struck him that his daughter, more than his son, missed her mother the most. She needed a mom to guide her through her trying teens, not a father who had no idea what to with an emotional girl.

He put his dishes in the autowasher, noticing again a chill.

Really need to check the heating system.

He retreated to his bedroom after taking a quick hot shower. All the used water would be recycled into the hydroponics, which supplied both their fresh air along with vegetables and fruit. Josh tended the garden between reading and his studies.

Crawling underneath the covers, Peter quickly fell asleep, a habit he'd gotten into after years in the Space Service. Never knew when he might be awakened for some ship emergency.

He awoke to his daughter's horrific scream. Peter scrambled for his well-worn gray sweats and stepped barefoot out onto the icy deck. Maisy lay in a crumbled heap outside her bedroom, her body shaking uncontrollably. At least she'd put a fluffy robe on. Her nightgowns were skimpy and more revealing than a girl of her age should wear.

"What's all the excitement?" Josh asked, stifling a yawn. He looked much younger than his seventeen years in bright red shorts and a blue T-shirt.

"Take care of your sister," Peter ordered as he stepped past his daughter. He entered her room. The first thing he noticed was the extreme cold. Ice hugged the ceiling and edged the small oval mirror hanging on the wall. Briefly he thought he saw a misty figure bending over the bed. It turned its 'head' toward him.

He heard a loud yowl and a growling hiss. Cali appeared from nowhere, her white fur puffed, her ears back. Her brown and orange-splotched tail twitched angrily.

Okay. Not my imagination.

The mist squiggled back, clung to the wall and vanished under the ice. After several seconds the room returned to normal temperature, the melting ice leaving wet streaks on the walls.

"Josh! Bring me some rags!" He scooped up the angry cat and set her outside. His son pushed something at him. He used it to wipe up the mess. Back in the narrow hallway, Josh looked quizzically at him.

"Where's Maisy?"

His son inclined his head downstairs. "Having another cup of hot chocolate and squeezing the cat." Josh frowned. "Where'd Cali come from?"

"No idea." He went into the small bathroom and tossed the rags into the recycler. He washed his hands and looked at his face. Fine lines were beginning to appear in the corners of his blue eyes. His brown hair had a few streaks of gray and his normally olive skin seemed a bit pale.

"So," Josh lounged on the door jamb. "What was it this time? More bad dreams? Or a bid for attention?"

Peter shook his head. "I think something was in her room."

"Like what?" The teen seemed to perk up.

I'm not superstitious. Or at least Peter hoped he wasn't. "No idea." He stepped out of the bathroom.

"We got an alien visitor?" Josh asked hopefully as he followed Peter back to the hallway.

"It was a ghost," Maisy said. She stood a few feet away, her mug griped in one hand, her pink robe tightly belted to her maturing body.

Josh rolled his eyes. Every time Peter looked at his son he saw a reflection of his wife. He even had her dark skin and matching wiry hair.

"There's no such thing." Peter had to keep her imagination in check. He also didn't want them all jumping at every unexpected creak or shadow.

Maisy snorted. She grabbed Cali, who protested being picked up. "Believe what you want. I know what I saw." She marched back into her room. The door hissed closed.

"Think she'll be okay in there?" Josh pointed at the closed door. "We could always switch."

"She's got Cali." Why did he think the cat would be any type of protection?

Josh narrowed his eyes. "You really think we have a ghost, Dad?"

"I don't believe in ghosts."

"Yeah. Right." Josh shrugged and headed for his room. "I'm

gonna read for a while."

"Try to get some sleep." Peter watched as the door slid shut. He looked from one child's room to the other before going back to his own.

For a long, long time he stared into the darkness, his mind speculating on what he'd seen. He'd heard about and experienced many strange things in space. They'd gotten explained away as new legends or old myths. He suspected some held an element of truth, while others no doubt had been pure fabrication. The tales he'd listened to had helped him pass time during the long voyages.

Peter's grandfather had told him tales about lighthouses, being one of the last keeper's himself. Some had been about ghosts, others about the life he'd led. Many times he'd regretted never recording them. It was part of Josh and Maisy's past and they should know where they came from.

With their family's history, being the first keeper to occupy the Pluto lighthouse seemed natural. He certainly didn't intend to begin or end his watch by beginning any ghost stories.

He shuddered as the room's temperature dropped. He forced his eyes closed. *There's nothing there.*

~ * ~

His dreams had him hunting rats in stinky places and suffocating in a blanket. He started awake, surprised to find Cali sprawled on his chest. Her paw rested gently on his cheek, reminding him of his wife's thin fingers.

"How'd you get in here?" Cali opened one yellow eye to look at him before closing it again. "You need to move." Her response was to start purring. "I mean it."

He started to sit up. The cat gave him a disgusted look and reluctantly moved to curl up at the end of his bed. Her tail flicked in agitation. "I warned you."

Peter dressed in his uniform. Not that he really needed to wear it every day, just if a ship stopped. The habit gave him a sense of security and normalcy. Something he badly needed since his wife's death had upset his routine and life.

Thinking of her made his chest freeze up. He pushed aside the strong urge to return to bed. If he did, he'd never get up again.

Josh and Maisy need me he reminded himself.

Peter took a deep breath and went to find breakfast. Josh sat at the table nibbling on dry cereal, reading yet another comic book. This one had blue costumed characters on it, one of which was covered by rock. "How are your studies going?" He made instant coffee, dumped sugar in it and tossed eggs into the zap.

"Okay." Josh turned the page, popping another sugary bite into his mouth.

"Where's your sister?" He sat down, placing his plate on the table and taking another sip to help him wake up.

"Still sleeping."

"I'd appreciate it if you made sure Maisy got her lessons done."

"She won't listen to me, but I'll try."

His sister probably wouldn't. *I need to sit down and have a talk with her. She needs new priorities. Not just how she looks.* "Thanks. I appreciate it."

"No prob, Dad." He turned another page.

Their shared silence had always been comfortable. Peter ate his spongy eggs and drank his passable coffee. He really didn't like instant, yet it was cheaper to ship than the real thing. He'd certainly drunk enough through the years.

A chill passed through the room. He glanced up. Josh shivered, but never looked up. A wispy figure twirled gracefully and darted through the wall.

I do NOT *believe in ghosts.*

Back in the light he went to work polishing the delicate surfaces. Periodically, he'd wince as icy air filtered through. The heating systems definitely needed to be checked.

Eventually, every mapped system would have their own lighthouse, or so it had been explained to him by his assignment officer. They were a stop gap measure until someone figured out how to accurately plot coordinates in a constantly expanding galaxy.

He stretched, feeling every muscle in his back and hated how old his body felt. A damp chill filled the air and he froze, his eyes darting around. Not far away a bipedal figure hovered, its 'head' darting this way or that, like it was trying to figure out something.

I don't believe in ghosts, he repeated to himself.

It noticed him, hobbling over to peer closely into his face. A dark circle mouth appeared and an ear shattering wail filled the confined space. Peter clamped his hands over his ears and stumbled down the stairs.

"What's that noise, Dad?" Josh's eyes were wide.

"No idea," he panted, glancing over his shoulder, hoping the noise would stop. A loud yowl reached his ears. He grabbed for Cali as she dashed up the stairs. Peter started to follow. Maisy would never forgive him if something happened to her cat.

"Dad!" Josh's hand shot out to stop him.

His hand had grabbed Cali's tail when the cat simply vanished. His fingers closed on empty space. He stumbled, roughly bumping his knee on the hard metal. He bit back a cuss word.

"Dad?" Josh suddenly stood next to him.

The noise above stopped and a deafening quiet fell. "Stay here." Peter managed to limp upstairs. In the air hung a deep chill, their intruder gone. Where it had stood a congealed puddle of gel wobbled. He grabbed several rags and cleaned it up. What was going on and why?

And where in the stars had the cat gone?

He shook his head and gingerly made his way back downstairs. In the living area he checked his knee. Purple and blue splotches appeared.

"Better put some ice on that." Josh moved to the small freezer, removed several cubes and wrapped them in a towel. He pushed it into Peter's hands.

"Thanks." Peter sat at the table, feeling relief as the cold spread across his injured knee.

"Should put it up, too. It'll help the swelling."

"Where'd you learn that?" Peter eased his leg up onto another chair. It did help.

"Basic first aid." Josh puttered around the kitchen. Smells of chicken and hot chocolate filled the confined space. "Here." He put a plate down in front of Peter.

"Thanks."

"No prob." Josh sat down opposite his father. Peter noticed the heaping plate and the large mug of hot cocoa. "I think we have ghosts, Dad."

"There's no such things as ghosts." Peter cut into the chicken and forced himself to eat.

"You sure?" His son swallowed more cocoa before attacking

his lunch.

Was he? Peter couldn't explain the specters he'd seen any more than where the cat had vanished. He just hoped Maisy wouldn't pitch another hysterical fit when she learned her beloved Cali was once again missing.

Peter eased his injured knee into a more comfortable position and sampled the chicken. Its flavor reminded him of the meals his wife had prepared. He took another bite trying to decipher the secret ingredient.

"Chocolate," Josh said.

"What?" He looked up at his son.

"Mom used to add a tablespoon of cocoa to the chicken." Josh grinned. "Not to mention cayenne pepper."

"How do you know?"

Josh shrugged. His face briefly looked sad. "Used to watch her cook."

"I didn't know." Peter was stunned his son knew something he didn't.

"You were gone a lot."

Peter felt guilty about all that he'd missed.

"Done?"

Peter nodded.

Josh gathered up their dishes and put them in the sink to be cleaned later. He suspected his son would leave them for Maisy to put in the autowasher.

"Something smells good."

Glancing behind him, he saw his daughter standing there. She'd put on some leopard spotted outfit. The only thing missing were a tail and ears. Peter had a twinge of guilt over the missing Cali.

"You look silly." Josh sat down and picked up a comic book.

She stuck her tongue out at him. "What's to eat?"

"Left you a plate in the zap." Josh opened the pages, pretending to ignore his sister. Peter didn't miss the teen's watchful eyes as she warmed her food. She sat down and took a bite. "Tastes like mom used to make," she said. Her brother grinned proudly.

"Your brother is a good cook."

"Yeah, sometimes."

Peter shook his head and decided to test his knee. It hurt when he put weight on it.

"Better keep it iced and elevated all day," Josh suggested.

"I have work to do."

"Dad, you can't do your job if you're hurt."

Maisy demanded, "What happened?"

"We had another ghost while you were asleep," Josh answered.

His daughter shivered. "I thought the only haunted light-houses were back on Earth."

"There's no such things as ghosts," Peter snapped, immediately regretting it by the look of hurt on her face.

"Ah, come on, Dad." Josh closed his comic book. "You yourself told us stories about the strange things you'd seen out in space. Mom, too."

"They're just stories made up to entertain or explain…"

"…the unexplainable," Josh finished. "Yeah, so mom said, too."

Peter saw his daughter's hand dart out to grab her brother's arm. Her frightened eyes looked toward the stairs. Slowly, he turned to see what had scared her.

A shadow hovered there. Yet, something about this one seemed familiar. Maybe it was the tilt of the head or cascade of dark wiry hair or the warm brown eyes he'd seen every day they'd been together.

"Holy Three, no," he choked out.

Chairs scratched across the metal floor. Peter averted his gaze. Looking at anywhere was better than staring into those all too familiar and loving eyes.

Both of his children huddled together, Josh's arm around his younger sister.

"Madhur?" Peter whispered.

Slowly the figure faced him, sadness reflected on the ghostly pale face. At her feet Cali suddenly appeared, rubbing against what should have been his wife's legs.

"Where'd Cali come from?" Maisy demanded.

"No idea." Peter put his ice pack on the table and stood up, using the smooth top to steady himself.

"What's going on, Dad?" Josh's voice squeaked.

"I don't know."

His wife's form whirled like a snake around a branch. She floated downstairs. Cali dashed after her.

"Stay here," Peter ordered. He grimaced as he put weight on his leg. Somehow he limped down the stairs into the console room, surprised to find the com on, the stars sparkling through the one window staring out into space.

A message scrolled across. *I'm dead.*

"I know." The pain of her loss ripped across his heart and all his defenses he'd kept up snapped. He sank into the chair before the screen, his body shaking.

I wanted to come home.

Peter couldn't answer. He felt as if the air had been sucked out, replaced by vacuum, and he choked.

Cali leaped up on the console. Her purr filled the room.

His uncomprehending eyes stared at the cat then his shadow wife.

Please. She extended her hand. He could see through it and his dam of grief burst. "No!" Peter fell to his knees, not even flinching at the unexpected sharp pain.

His wife kneeled before him, her phantom silky fingers brushing against his cheek.

"Mom!" Maisy screamed, tears streaking down her cheeks.

When had Josh and Maisy come down?

Take care of your father. She opened her arms and both her children ran into them. Peter couldn't move.

Cali chirped inquisitively. His wife's ghost released her children, a sad smile on her full lips.

I'm going home now. Her white mist form oozed through the wall, briefly pausing before the window.

"Wait!" he screamed. Peter staggered to his feet. His fingers splayed on the thick glass.

Madhur raised her hand in a final goodbye. She churned as she headed out into the blackness.

The cat urped, bumping against his legs.

His shocked mind registered his children against him, one on each side. Peter's cheek rested on Maisy's silky hair and his son secure against his chest. Their grief and loss bonded them together and made them the one thing he'd longed for since he'd returned from space—a family again.

Later, after Josh and Maisy slept in their rooms, Cali at her rightful place at the foot of his daughter's bed, Peter sat down to make his first official log entry. It wouldn't matter if the next keeper believed it or not. His story would be added to the annuals of the unexplained and would be told many times by future keepers.

He finished his entry and smiled at the memory of his wife's fingers against his cheek. Peter touched the spot. There would always be a longing in his soul but in time, his heart would heal.

He stared at the simple words at the end of his ghostly tale.

A lighthouse has always been the beacon to sailors at sea, and other travelers who longed to reach distant shores. Here in space, that is true as well, welcoming our long lost home.

A black hole sits in the center of the Milky Way Galaxy. What an interesting idea to write a poem about. The editor who originally published thought it good enough that it was nominated for the Rhysling award for Science Fiction Poetry.

Welcomed Cast Outs

Blackness.
We came from there.
The dark, dark, whirling center of the galaxy
where stars circle its greedy heart
before they're devoured.

Is it any wonder we're predators?

Pointy ears which hear what you can not.
Sharp claws to shred our prey
or maybe your arm, toe, or foot.
The bittersweet taste of blood
our dessert and right.

Yet, you cuddle our furred bodies,
pet our snake-shaped heads,
let us sleep on your shredded couch,
warm chair, and snuggly bed.

Night.
Our time.
So like our ancient home.
Time to hunt and play, keep you awake
with our games of tag and pouncing.

Day.
Time to sleep.
Sometimes ask for a pet.
Mostly ignore you.

Or watch the winged things land, eat,
on metal or wooded houses,
so like your own.

Dana Bell

We wish to chase the bushy tailed ones
who eat the seeds and peanuts
you put outside for them
on the white snow
or in the tall green grass.

Grass.
The perfect place
for us to wait,
to hunt them.

Instead,
clear glass separates us
from our rightful prey.

Cat TV you tell us.

Yet,
Do you not wonder
how we came into your world?

We know the historical records suggest
it was the storage bins of Egypt
that lured us to you.

After all,
there were hungry rats,
a plentiful food source
for us.

Silly humans.
Not truly how we came into your world.

You see,
the deadly heart cast us out.
We were too dangerous
and rivaled its power.

There was this portal,
a straw bag
filled with the dust of the desert,
gnawed on bones,
unfulfilled, lost dreams.

We found it,
entered your realm.
The rightful new hunters
and rulers.

You welcomed us.
Foolish humans.

Humans have their version of what happened in the Garden of Eden. And the cats have theirs as shared in The Cat's Creation Tale.

The Cat's Creation Tale

"In the land where the river overruns the bank and brings prosperity, in the land ruled over by the burning sun and sands, in the land where we were first birthed, comes the tale I will you, my dears."

The storytellers' voice carried over the roar of the falls and I pause by the white blossomed bush, my tail slowly weaving back and forth. I hadn't wanted to be late, but my human had gone to bed late. When I was certain she was fast asleep, I crept out the open window and made my way here.

It had taken longer than I wanted, as there are many dangers in this wild land so close to town. There are those with the horns and the sharp whistles during their time of mating who could trample on us with their sharp hooves or those like us only larger for which we would make an excellent meal for or the cream-colored canines we avoided for the same reason.

Before my night adjusted eyes I could see the honored Weaver of Tales, sitting high upon a white granite boulder. She was tan colored with spots gracing her fur, a high Lady of the Old Lands.

"For it is by our claws Apophis was brought down, not left to wander on his belly, as is the popular mythos of those who have no true understanding of knowledge."

I heard the rerows of the younglings. They've not heard this tale before. If I could have smiled as my human did, I would have done so.

Looking around I could see every feline from town and the ranches as well as the wild ones. They were scattered about on boulders or the paved paths that were put there for human feet. Some were sitting, others lying on their bellies, all their bright eyes focused on our honored guest.

Quickly I made my way to sit beside Grazer. He's all gray with bright yellow eyes. He's lived with his human a long time in the neighboring house. I hunt the mice who torment him because he no longer can catch them.

He saw me and greeted me with a faint rumble.

"Of what do I speak? Yes, I see the question in your eyes. The yearning to know the secret I shall impart upon you, but as all tales do, there is a beginning."

She paused again, lifting a dainty paw to clean between her claws. When she finished she spoke again. *"Our second ancestress lived in the palace of the Pharaoh. Hers was a place of high honor for she sat upon a silk cushion at his sandaled feet. He called her Bast, out of respect for the one worshiped, who brought fertility upon the humans and upon their gods as well."*

Almost, I could hear laughter in her tone.

"They had many beliefs in the land of our birth, mixed with those of yet another people for whom our first ancestress did a great favor."

First ancestress? Her reference caught my attention. Many times I'd heard of the second, but never the first.

"While sitting at Pharaoh's feet, our second ancestress told a story to her young. Not that the Ruler of Two Lands understood it, of course, for they had their own version.

She told her young of the Earth and Sky, twins, a brother and sister, and the great romance between them. The Sun, being a jealous one, for Sky was his wife, separated them.

When Sky mated with her brother Earth, her husband put a curse upon her. She was never to have children while he put light in the sky.

So great was her sadness that she cried and cried and cried."

A lamenting cry echoed into the night from all the shes. I heard it deep within my bones and understood their sorrow. Although I am a male, I have been changed, by my human's design. I, too, know a deep loss.

"Another of the ancient gods, although in the human tale he was one and the same and how he could play checkers against himself and win, is, shall we say, beyond belief, took a small portion of light and made five new days so Sky could have five children.

But this is an untruth, my dears. What truly happened is Bast took pity upon poor Sky and poured fertility upon her, despite her jealous husband's curse.

And so did Sky have her five children."

The crying call of the large one like us echoed through the moon filled black followed by the shrill scream of the long ear dying. At least none of us would fill its belly. This time.

"Perhaps strangest of all is the name of one of the sons, the third I believe, was Set, so similar to Seth, as was Adam's and Eve's third son. Set was an evil child who murdered his brother. Every night he became the great serpent who battled against Sun.

He even fought his own brother Horus. It was a fight between good and evil. Much like God and his fallen angel Lucifer, for all must have the choice and the right to decide for themselves. Set would have died had not Isis, his sister, taken pity on him and spared his <u>life.</u> There was a heartbeat before she spoke again. *"So she kept chaos upon the land. Or so goes the story the ancient ones told.*

Our second ancestress dealt with Set. Those silly pictures you see of us using a knife to kill him are ridiculous. Why do we need human steel when we were born with deadly claws?"

Yowls filled the area overpowering the waterfall. I added my voice to theirs.

Somewhere in the valley the yipping howls of the canines answered. It seems they need so little to make noise and announce their presence. It must make it difficult for them to hunt. Perhaps that is why the small ones like them disappear regularly in the town. They are easier prey because they are not so bright.

Or perhaps it is their humans who are not.

"Then one day, came one before Pharaoh demanding the freedom of his people. He smelled of wooly and did not bow before the Great One.

Our second ancestress was furious at the insult.

Wooly Smell spoke his words and left, leaving the Pharaoh angry.

So did she follow him to the land of Goshen to see what mischief stirred. In their hovels she heard yet another tale, a tale of the beginning, for it was done by the hand of their God with no name.

He made the Heaven and Earth. He made the Land and Water. He made plants, animals and all else. And finally, in the end, He made man and woman. It was said He brought the animals to man to see what they should be called."

As if we, the People of the Night, would need humans to do such things for us. It was an offensive idea.

I snapped at a fly who kept buzzing around my head. It went away and died by the paw of a youngling. Well, to the young, all are things are to be played with. If it is alive so much the better, for so begins the skills of hunt, kill and eat.

"When our second ancestress heard this story, she did not know what to

think. So she left the land of Goshen, left the comfort of Pharaohs' palace and went on a great journey. Long did she travel the sands, finding respite only at the water places.

Humans often took pity on her and gave her meat from their plates and water from their wells. She sometimes slept in their tents, but more often, behind a rock or under a bush. Her journey went on and on. Sun passed through the Sky and Moon lit her way in the night. Until at last, she came to the place where four rivers met. It was a place long forgotten. A place of beginnings.

She stood on her tired and bleeding paws beside the bank and called. She did not know the name to call, but deep inside, she knew it was what she had to do."

The pines lining the falls swayed and whispered. They too, must be enraptured by the Storytellers tale. I laid down, and tucked my front paws under my brown body. I waited, as did us all.

"From across the river came an answering call. One, not unlike the second ancestress, only larger with fur as black as the night and eyes golden like the sun.

'Why do you come here?' asked she, who could be no other than the first ancestress.

'I seek you.'

'For what purpose?'

'Knowledge.'

'Come then.'

Our second ancestress could see no way to cross the great river. 'How do I come?' she asked.

'Have you no faith? Simply walk across.'

This was such a surprising answer, what else could she do but obey? Carefully, for our kind do not care to get wet, she crossed the water with dry paws.

On the other side, the great black lady followed a well-worn path into such trees as none had ever seen. In the very center stood two of great beauty and our second ancestress could only stare in wonder.

'You have not heard of these,' the first ancestress said. There was no surprise in her words.

'I have not.'

I too, had not heard this tale and hissed at the youngling who batted at my tail. Two startled blue eyes met mine before it hurried back to its mother side.

'These are the Trees of Life and of Knowledge and I remember well the day He of No Name placed them here.'

Our second ancestress was so startled she did not know how to answer.

'I remember, too, the day man came here and what he was told.' First Ancestress' tail switched back and forth. 'And when woman was brought.'

My human goes to church in town. I know sometimes men blame women for the evil and sin that came into the world. Yet, from these words, were we being told the blame given was true?

'They lived in the garden and cared for it, until the day the wily one came. Oh, he did not come just once, but many times.' Our first ancestress flexed her claws. 'I saw him and hissed and tried to warn them.'

'Warn them of what?'

'Do you not think I knew Set when I saw him?'

Set? wondered our second ancestress. What had a god of Egypt to do with the God of No Name and His people who seemed to think they wished freedom from Pharaoh?

'He crawled into this tree.' First Ancestress went to the larger of the two. Huge branches spread out and it seemed to overpower the smaller one. Its fruit was fuzzy, a rich pink in color, and seemed to hang tantalizing close, so easy to pick. 'He spoke to woman for many days, asking her questions, luring her in.

I rubbed against her bare legs, begging like a canine,' the words were spat out, 'for a pat on my head. I stood under the tree and yowled. The serpent taunted me by striking at me, but never marked me. I was too fast for him.'

I heard a fish plop in the water. I never hunted them, but I had seen humans dangle string with a worm on it trying to. I preferred mine in a can my person gave me.

Sometimes. Even I like raw, juicy meat fresh from a kill.

'Then came the day when she was picking fruit for their meal. He began speaking to her again. Changing the words the God of No Name had spoken. I tried yet again to interrupt, yet I could not.

What made me even more angry is that her husband, Adam, stood right there beside her and listened to the lies as well, just like he had—every time.

And when Eve reached up to pick the fruit, he didn't try to stop her. He let her disobey the God of No Name. They both sunk their puny teeth into the fruit, ate it, and then they both knew Good and Evil.'

The First Ancestress snorted like the hippos on the Nile. 'So Adam became like Set, and is, in my opinion, the true bringer of chaos.'

Light began to streak the sky against the clouds coming over the mountain. The buglers came to the river's edge to drink and overhead, the great flyer passed several times.

I knew it was time for us to return to our homes and our humans. We were much wiser now for knowing the truth and sad we could not share it. I saw others like myself get to their paws preparing to leave.

"One final thing you must know, my dears."

We all stopped to listen, for we did not know when the storyteller would come again.

'Our second ancestress asked one final question. Why are you still in the garden and why have you not ventured to the land of the sands and the flooding river?'

There was a long silence and she began to think her question would not be answered. She turned to again cross the river and return to Pharaohs' palace.

'This is my reward,' the First Ancestress replied.

'For trying to stop Set and Adam and Eve?'

'Not exactly.'

'What then? Tell me so I might tell my young, and they theirs, for all our days.'

With glowing golden eyes the First Ancestress gazed up into the branches of the tree. *The human version says the serpent was cursed by the God of No Name to crawl upon his belly and eat dust and be an enemy of woman.'*

The great flyer gave his cry as he disappeared over the tops of the pines. I was relieved. I had heard sometimes, he took one of us as meat.

"Is that the end of the story?" one of the younglings asked.

I think if the Storyteller could have smiled, she would have. *"No, my dears."* And her body began to fade as the sunlight struck it. *"The answer the First Ancestress gave me as we spoke in the garden was this,"* and her voice began to fade and drift back through the whispers of the past, *"Set will never again trouble Eve or her children. Our First Ancestress, even then, knew how to use her claws."*

The editor who accepted this story wrote a most interesting compliment. She didn't like vampire stories, but accepted Oasis because it took a creative angle on an old theme and did something new with it.

Oasis

Tangy, salty blood poured over my tongue, rolling warmly down my throat, through my stomach and into my veins. The howl of the jackal filled the desert night and my pointed ears twitched. My prey flopped one last time and lay still. I dropped it. It couldn't even be tossed into the air and batted around as was proper.

Lifting my head, I listened for answering canine cries and was reassured by the silence. There were no packs about. Slowly I padded across the cooling sands, my tail straight up, my whiskers twitching. Not far away were the brackish waters of a long-abandoned oasis. I could hear the long green palms rattling and a coconut splot as it hit the ground.

I had been here a long time. Alone. Forgotten. Even by the one who had made me.

Not that her act was a cruel one. To be a Chosen One was an honor. It meant I got to live longer than my mortal life.

I couldn't complain though. My mortal life had been good. I'd been pampered and loved by the mistress of the house and the hunting companion for her first-born son. I'd laid many captured prey at his feet and the feast that followed had always been filling.

Until the day a crocodile had pulled me under the murky depths of the Nile. When I next opened my brown eyes, I had been surrounded by more of my kind than I could count. Around me had been a great temple, cool breezes snapping sheer white fabric as it hung from the ceiling. In the center was a huge golden soft pillow and on it, sat the most beautiful female I had ever seen.

"Welcome," her purring voice had greeted me.

I knew who she was. My house mistress had kept a small shrine in her chambers. She often prayed to the goddess for fertility and children.

Slowly I dropped to my belly. It was the proper way to greet Bast.

"There is no need Hunter. You died with dignity as befitted your station."

By being swallowed by a crocodile? I had not agreed.

Her low purr filled the air. "You are home. Come, sit beside me."

I'd risen to my paws and hesitantly crossed the stone floor. Furred bodies scattered, a few kittens tumbling over each other. I'd stopped before the goddess. It had not felt right sitting beside her.

"I am unworthy," I had told her.

"Not so." Her golden eyes blinked. She'd licked a spot on her tan shoulder. I could not help but think how perfect her black spots were.

Another male entered, his huge body dominating the temple. Many stopped their antics to sit and stare at him. I'd seen the flicking tails, the females who rubbed against him.

"Who is that?" I'd asked.

"A Chosen One."

A Chosen One! My dame had told me stories about them before I had been taken from her. I'd always thought there was more to our history than the tales the humans told of us. How we'd come to them by protecting their granaries. How they'd welcomed us and taken us into their homes.

They'd built temples to the goddess. Given her a city— Bubastis. A festival. Thousands attended. How many children had been born as a result? I do not think even the humans knew.

He'd stopped before her, tall, proud. He was tan like her, with black spots, his brown eyes respectful. "I have come, as you asked."

"So you have brave Warrior." She turned to look at me. "This one I have long watched. He will be a new Chosen One."

Me? What had I done to earn such an honor?

"You will instruct him," she'd continued.

The other male had blinked.

She'd risen, stretching her limber body. Such a body any male would yearn for. Her black nose touched mine. "When you wake, you will know hunger. Aritu will be your guide."

Guides to the underworld I knew. Yet, I knew it was not the same.

"Sleep now," she'd urged.

A languid feeling surged through my body. Slowly I dropped to the hard stone. I could not keep my eyes open. My legs collapsed and a cold I had not even felt in death filled me. When I awoke, my guide Aritu was with me.

"I am to teach you how to hunt your prey. How to live among the humans and not be discovered."

"I know how to live among humans," I hissed.

"As you once were yes. Not now."

Skitter. Skitter.

My hunger awoke full force. I pounced upon the creature, tearing it apart, the warm life it had once held now dripping into my mouth.

"Not bad for your first kill," Aritu said. "Next time, you need only tear its neck open." He looked upon the torn flesh and fur scattered among the green reeds. "The humans will think a hawk took it."

"What does it matter what they think?" I sat and cleaned blood from around my mouth. My tongue savored the flavor.

"They have their own stories about blood drinkers." He looked away. "I do not think you would care to die by fire.'

Fire. Nesert. That would be a good name for me in this new life. I stared across the shivering greens. "How long will you stay with me?"

"Until you know what you need to live your new life fully."

His instruction had taken a short time, three turns of the full moon. It seemed I learned quickly and well. I was careful with my kills, only killing the pests around the houses, those with the deadly slithering bite and sometimes, the croaking ones. I always left their bodies hidden, sometimes burying them as if they were disgusting and smelly.

I soon learned the mortal felines, would hiss and run away from me. Although we were revered, we were also feared. No female would allow me to approach so I began to wander, as males are known to do. Away from the royal city and villages I traveled, even away from the well-worn caravan trails. When I found this place after many, many, many sunsets, I stayed. It had become home to me.

There was always prey. The water attracted despite the stale smell. The dry of the desert drove them to it. They could not help themselves. Their thirst was a wild thing.

Almost as wild as mine.

As the long nights dragged one into the next to the next, I began to wonder if this had been the fate the goddess meant for me. Why had she picked me to be a Chosen One yet ignored me beyond allowing the brief companionship of Aritu? Not that males often chose to travel together.

"Why am I here?" I asked her. I did not expect an answer.

Overhead the great owl hooted and a jackal moaned. There was no other noise. I was alone. I sank upon the sand the grit working into my fur and irritating my skin.

"What honor is there in being a Chosen One?" I yowled into the bright dark. There was a full orange moon caressing the black. I believe it was the time of Halloween, a new holiday those of this day celebrated.

"So you are a Chosen One."

I jumped to my paws, my fur puffed up. I hissed at the intruder I had not heard approach.

Out from the tree shadows she emerged. Another of my kind, her fur black like the night yet I could see the darker spots smattered upon her body. Her thin tail moved slowly from side to side.

"You question the honor Bast bestowed upon you?" Her eyes were bright sun yellow.

How could I answer a female as beautiful as she? And one who did not run from me. Yet as the wind shifted I caught the scent of her. There was no mistaking it. We Chosen Ones do not smell as those who are mortal.

"You know." She sat upon her haunches, her tail daintily draped over her front paws.

"How did you come to be here?" I growled at her.

If she could have shrugged as the humans do, I believe she would have. Instead, she blinked, her eyes vanishing into darkness before returning again. "I wandered. As did you."

"You chose ill." I padded away toward the water. I did not truly want her company.

"I chose well." Her voice carried over the distance as if she traveled beside me.

I stopped, turning my head to stare at her. She sat where I had left her.

"I am hungry and if you do not mind sharing your territory, I would like to hunt."

Did I mind? I didn't know. I sneezed and trotted to the far side of the shore. She could have that side.

~ * ~

When Ra again rose from the underworld bathing the land in this brilliant glory, I retreated to the piled stones where I always slept the day away. I had no idea where the female had gone. My eyes closed and my body rested until Ra battled below.

The near full moon hung in the sky. Its light was welcome but I really didn't need it. An asp glided near daring to try and strike. It died quickly, its reptilian blood bitter and filling. I tossed it aside and looked around for the female. Had she stayed? Or had she traveled on?

"You found a good sleeping spot."

I jumped and whirled, hissing at her. I hated she could approach and I not hear her.

"You do not have to be alone."

"Our kind is always alone."

Her pink tongue darted out and she cleaned blood off her fur. "Not always."

"I was a great hunter." Now why had I told her that?

Her purr was quiet. I had to listen very hard to hear it. "From how quickly you killed the poison one, I would have guessed that."

"And you?"

She blinked. "I was in the temple."

I knew of temple cats. They'd been well cared for. Or so I'd heard. Darker rumors about their fate had reached my ears as well.

"How did you come to the goddess and become a Chosen One?" I was curious. I sat in the still warm sand, my tail behind me and still.

"I was the chosen sacrifice." Her body shuddered. "The priests made my death as painless as possible but as I parted from my body I saw what they did." She looked toward the moon. "I was told afterward they wrapped me, anointing my remains with oils and perfumes."

So, the rumors I'd heard were true. If so, why had the goddess once allowed the priests to kill her own?

"When I awoke, I was with Bast." Her gaze returned to me. "She did not say what had been done with me. Instead, she offered me the greatest honor."

"To become a Chosen One." Aritu had told me the goddess only transformed males. "But I thought," I began.

"She chose only males?" She lifted her back leg and scratched her ear. "Mostly. Males will protect what is hers."

"Protect?" I was puzzled.

"You will learn," she stopped. "What do you call yourself?"

"Nesert."

"Nesert. Fire. A good choice."

"I will learn what?"

"The goddess has good reason for those she chooses. No doubt a day will come when she will call upon you to accomplish some task for her."

"I can think of no task the goddess would ask of me."

"I would not be so certain." She stretched, her limbs long and lithe. "I know of one who often came to the temple and took away some of the kittens. The priests were furious and terrified."

Since we were considered sacred, I could understand the priests fear. They could have been put to death if it could be proven their negligence had caused the kittens to perish.

"Where did he take them?"

"I don't know. I dared to ask him once. He said simply he had been told to take them to the homes of those who were true worshippers of the goddess. The kittens would be quite safe and well cared for."

I wondered at this. How had the goddess known which humans could be trusted with such a responsibility?

"There is no doubt she will one day have such a task for you, Nesert."

"What are you called?" I dared to ask.

"Hetep."

Her name meant peace and aptly so. I felt calmer and relaxed around her. She would never challenge me for what was mine.

"We could share this place." She waited in silence for my answer.

"Perhaps." I was not certain I wished to give up my self-imposed solitude.

"I tire of wandering." She sank down, tucking her front paws up under her body. "It would be good to have a place to hunt away from the humans."

"I have found it so."

"Most males do."

At least she understood that about us. Strange how some of our nature remained while other parts of it fled. "I would not mind if you stayed." Perhaps I did truly tire of being alone.

"I would glad to." She blinked, her eyes the only sun I would see for many, many, many moons.

Little One, 19, and Tabitha, 18, died a year and half apart. Chandra's Gift expressed the grief of losing two long time companions, and some of what happens in this tale, is true.

Chandra's Gift

'Merow'

I sat up in bed, my eyes darting around the fireplace lit room. The faint light flickered off the plain dirt walls and nothing moved in my cottage. Quickly my hand darted to my side and upon finding it empty, I again swallowed tears as they threatened to choke me. My small longtime companion was in truth gone.

Slowly I eased myself down onto the hard cot, pulling the coarse fabric over my chilled body. For one such as myself, used to the best of what my world had to offer, living in such poverty was not something I relished. However, with death stalking the cities and byways, my being here was much safer.

A crackling from the fire drew my attention. Bright orange glowed in the embers below and a few yellow flames still flickered. Still, the chill of the night enclosed about me and uneasily I fell back to sleep.

With the morning came the full realization I was indeed, alone. Two small bowls still sat in their place of honor next to the back door and I had not the heart to remove them. I began my daily routine by washing my face and hands in the cold water from the well. I dried them with my kerchief, one of the few luxuries I still had.

From the window looking out over the sharp white cliffs, I could see Fall had peaked and the first touches of Winter had begun to enshroud the land. Rusty leaves littered my small now empty garden space. Well, not totally empty. A small mound sat to one side and I knew under the hard earth Chandra slumbered the sleep from which none of us wake.

Tears threatened yet again and I angrily dashed them away. There was the morning porridge to cook, and bread to bake, and a dozen other tasks that now made up my day. I used to take the presence of servants for granted. Now I understood their hard life.

The sun crossed the sky as it did every day of my exile. I heard no hooves on the sparse cobble outside my cottage nor even the cry of a falcon. At dusk I went to the small barn and fed my horse, wondering how I would survive the long winter. I patted the soft long nose and again pondered the idea of freeing Levi for the season. Perhaps he would live longer if he were free to range and graze. Or perhaps not. He had never known any type of care except what had been given him.

Carefully I closed the barn door to return to the cottage. Several leaves danced under the wind's direction and clung to my long, tattered skirts. I brushed at them hoping they would remain outside. I needed nothing else to clean this day.

'Merow.'

The cry caused me to stop in my tracks. My eyes found Chandra's grave. None of the dirt was disturbed. The wilted flowers I had placed there at the beginning of the Summer had not moved, despite the weather's best efforts.

"You're just lonely," I told myself. My voice sounded rusty from long nonuse. I had not spoken much since death had taken my one companion.

I hurried back into my home. I tried to forget the haunting cry. I fried potatoes adding a touch of rosemary. I had dried the fragrant plant earlier in the week. The stone container holding the leaves sat upon a shelf with all the others I had worked on. The rest of what I had harvested sat on high shelves out of the reach of vermin. Chandra had kept their numbers low. Now I feared I might starve since I had seen beady red eyes watching me from under the low branches of the trees. They would try to come in when the snow began to fall.

Long did I sit by the fire in my only chair. In my lap rested the ancient book of the God I had been taught to fear as a child. As I read the familiar passages, I found not the terror of a vengeful, angry deity, but one of compassion and love. It brought to mind the one question I had yet to discover an answer to.

"Where is Chandra? Is she in heaven with you?"

My whisper seemed to fill the room. Pops and sizzles replied. The drowsy heat filled my body and I put the book aside to crawl under the meager covers of my bed. My eyes closed upon another day and opened when a new one began. My routine was the same and so drifted the last of Fall into the cold and snow of Winter.

I had taken to keeping the axe next to my bed and listening through the long dark nights for the scuttle of tiny feet or something shifting on my shelves. How many of the rats I killed I do not know. I only know I constantly wished Chandra was still with me to deal death to them.

The time of Yule Log approached and my thoughts constantly returned to the grand celebrations of my father's house. I would have none this year. My feast consisted of dried fruit and a meager potato.

Again I took my book and read the story I had heard all my life, the time of taxes and a couple riding to his hometown, about the star, the wise men and the child born. When I finished I sat trying not to shiver for cold had invaded and was so deep I seemed never to be warm.

'Merow'.

I started awake unaware I had slept. My back and neck hurt from the angle forced upon them by the chair back. The fire was dangerously low and I hastily added more fuel. I hoped the storm raging outside subsided in the morning for I had great need to chop more. My failure to stock enough during the warm months now cost me precious daylight I needed for other tasks.

Glancing around my cottage and I began to fear I was losing my sanity. How many times had I heard Chandra's cry? And why did I hear her when I knew she was dead and buried?

"Why, God?" I gasped out as tears once again flooded by cheeks. I jumped up as I felt a bit of fur brush my ankle. "What?" Fearfully I looked down afraid to see a rat had crept upon me while I slept.

Instead I briefly saw the shadow of a proud brown and black tail and I knew to whom it belonged. My thankful heart knew peace and acceptance of my companion's loss. My tears changed from sadness to joy and I accepted the gift I had been given.

Shadow is a fun little Halloween trick played on humans by a cat who is a Chosen One.

Shadow

"Arrrooohhh!"

The lonely wolf cry bounced through the mountain valley, answered by the rest of the pack. They lurked amongst the black snow tipped peaks. Their harmonious song caused Shadow to pause, one delicate paw raised as her ears twitched listening.

Not that she feared any attack from them. There were plenty of the Long Horns, or Elk, as the humans called them, for the pack to hunt. Her tiny body would not even fill one belly, let alone the many she knew there were.

Besides, she'd had a few encounters with the two dominates. Her scent had frightened them and sent them running for the safety of the forest. Now when they crossed her trail, they circled wide to avoid her.

How wise of them.

Shadow dared to cross the flat frozen area. Her nose told her there was a Long Horn with its young, the herd and the winning male not far away. During the time of the yellow and orange leaves before the first frost, the males had filled the air with their high-pitched calls, luring females for mating.

She no longer had any interest in such activities. Her desires had vanished long ago in the land of the Queen. Shadow had died by the hands of fanatics certain she was the familiar of a witch. The poor old woman who had sheltered her had been burned alive.

'And they think us vicious,' she accused those of long ago.

Wind danced along the valley floor bringing with it the smell of pines, Long Horn and other creatures who rightfully lived there. It also brought the smell of burning wood and the voices of humans.

She again stopped. Her head twisted in the direction of the humans.

They were dirty. They smelled of vile beer. She could taste the cigarettes on her pink tongue.

Her intention had been to cross the valley and disappear into the caves. Yet, the lurking danger the humans posed could not be passed by. Bast celebrated life. That was why she, Shadow, was a Chosen One.

She changed direction, her paws taking her toward the human camp and the dancing, popping fire. Their laughter drifted on the breeze caused by the farting and burping contest they seemed to be having. Nearby sat a light brown plastic container reeking of their waste.

Such disgusting creatures. Her kind buried their waste. How could they sleep near such stench? Or were their noses immune because of their so called 'intelligence'?

She stopped near the dark corner of one of their frail green tents. Inside were strewn articles of clothes, objects Shadow had no idea what they were used for, and their sleeping bags, also stinking of their sweat and pee.

Did they truly believe they could hunt their prey smelling as they did? Her ears told her the Long Horns were moving to the far end of the valley to avoid the humans.

"So," said one of the filthy men. "Anyone got a good Halloween story?"

One of their young moaned. Briefly, Shadow felt sympathy for it. "I'm gonna miss gettin' candy."

Another, who she assumed was its father, spoke up. "You can have candy anytime." He thumped his chest. "This is man bonding time."

They all laughed. Shadow narrowed her yellow eyes. They showed no sympathy for the suffering young.

"But I had my costume all picked out."

"Will you stop his complaining," a fat one griped.

A cloud passed over the full moon darkening the human camp. They all looked up before continuing to talk, burp and laugh.

Shadow no longer listened. She watched them as they drank and kept tossing their still lit cigarettes near the brittle dry grass. True, the time of frost had arrived, but all it took was one ash falling in the right place and the entire valley would burn.

It was her responsibility to stop them.

She waited until they were too drunk to really question what they saw. Since she'd been around humans for more than most of them had lived, she knew the moment.

Boldly she walked into their camp, puffing up her fur and yowling so loud the Long Horn far away broke into a run. The ground pounded with their fear.

"Look," the young pointed. "A cat!"

The grown ones stumbled about, many landing on the hard ground. Loud 'umpf's' escaped their mouths.

"That ain't no cat," the fat one said.

It was correct. She was not a 'cat'. Not as they knew them anyway.

She yowled again, allowing her eyes to flash red and her fangs to glitter in the fire's flame.

They screamed and ran for their trucks and SUV's. Doors slammed and motors sputtered. Rocks flew as they fled.

After they'd gone, Shadow returned to her normal appearance and gave herself a good wash. She settled down next to the dying fire, not that she really needed the warmth, and rested until the sun's first rays touched the gray sky.

Rising, she stretched making sure the fire was truly dead. Granted, a ranger would come and check. They always did. But as servant to the one who celebrated life, she would not abandon the campsite if it still burned.

Satisfied its embers were no danger, Shadow continued her path across the valley to the caves. On the way she startled a hopper, pounced on it, and drained its blood as it heart hammered in pure terror.

Such a delicious taste.

Mau's Mourn is completely based on Egyptian customs and how cats were reverently treated.

Mau's Mourn

Furred time during the reign of Pharoahs,
beside the bulging river of life, the Nile,
pillared city Bubastis raised to feline honor
priests to scratch ears and feed mice.

Bast, goddess, two proud forms,
human, keeper of dance and music,
feline, sleek black, necklace of precious gold,
protector of future human life.

Tawny cousin, Sekhmet,
roaring goddess of war,
chariot tossed mane flowing to saffron Ra,
spear claws shredding human prey.

Hieroglyphic faded image,
cherished cat's hunting on leash.
Honor wrapped mummies fertilized
English gardens.

No more ripped cloths and screams.
Sandy bones litter alleys.
Osiris walks in papyrus memory
Mau's mourn under the moonless desert night.

While the ancient Egyptians honored their dead felines, the same can not be said for those who discovered the cat mummies. They were brought back to England and sold as fertilizer. What happened is a loss to the historical community and disrespectful of those ancient beliefs. So the goddess Bast took her revenge in Night of Vengeance.

Night of Vengeance

In darkness her black paws padded through the moon lit English fields. Underneath she could feel them squirming, restless to be released. She stopped, wrapping her thin tail around her feet, her green eyes gazing through the tall wheat stalks. The wind caressed the golden grain causing a strange creaking, almost as if the locust of long ago were descending.

"It is time," she spoke to the soil. "Time to arise my beloved ones. Time to avenge what was unjustly done to you."

Shapes began to wriggle and crawl out of the ground. She could see their bound bodies and their wrapped tails angrily whipping. Painted eyes stared at her as they crept nearer.

"I have come with the blessings of Ra, Anubis, and my fierce cousin Sekhmet." She raised her proud head, the golden necklace she wore visible to all. "For this one night Anubis has granted you life. Use it well."

~ * ~

The guard entered the Egyptian display room in the Denver museum. Patrons wandered the semi-dark area, their talking a low familiar murmuring. He glanced at the various preserved mummies safe in their glass sealed coffins. Other items were there as well and his trained eye could tell nothing had been disturbed.

With a smile on his wrinkled face he turned to leave. It was time to check the next room.

A scream stopped him as a woman backed away from something near the far wall. Her male companion protectively stood in front of her.

"Now what?" the guard questioned as he hurried toward the

small crowd gathering. He hoped no one had broken an artifact. The museum director would be very angry if that had happened.

When he reached the area he skidded to stop and stared. The case containing the mummified cat had ruptured, sending glass splinters all over the tile floor. Standing in the center was a hissing, snarling feline, still covered in gauze.

It saw him and sprang. Shrieks of terror echoed and the last thing he saw was a pair of blazing painted eyes.

~ * ~

Nigel Metcalf heard scratching at the front door and grumbled as he forced himself out of bed. His wife of twenty years sighed and pulled the covers over her back. He knew she was used to him rising at odd hours. Often a sheep needed help with their birthing or a lamb had wandered off and needed rescuing.

He grabbed his wool coat and tossed it on before opening the front door. Nigel had expected Barry, his shepherd be there, instead, there seemed to be no one. In fact, he frowned worriedly. There wasn't any sound at all. The dog wasn't barking and not even the sheep were bleating.

A shiver ran through his body and he wished he was allowed to own a gun. But it was against the law in England and often a predator got away with a lamb or worse. Best he could do was inform the authorities and hoped they got the four-footed culprit.

"Best check," he said, grabbing a torch and going outside.

It was very dark. Darker than he'd ever seen it and so cold his breath felt like it was freezing on his face. He started across the yard to the barn when he thought he heard something. It sounded like crackling Fall leaves.

"Who's there?" he demanded, shining the torch all around.

Dozens of yellow eyes surrounded him.

"What?" He tried to back toward the house. The gathering mass surrounded him.

Their heads all turned and their bodies made a path for a pure, black cat, who leisurely strolled toward him. Although, looking at the feline, it wasn't much like any cat he'd ever seen. Not with those green eyes, the sleek body, and the gold necklace around its neck.

"Scat!" he shouted.

The cat's body shifted, blurred and before him stood a woman with a cat's face. She wore thin clothes and he wondered how her bare breasts couldn't be cold. Long fingers reached out and snagged his shoulder.

"Desecration," she hissed, although how she could talk through those nasty teeth were beyond him.

"Pardon?" Nigel had no idea what she was talking about.

"What was done to my people." Her other hand indicated the hundreds of cats.

"What's that got to do with me?"

"It was your kind who did this," she snarled.

He began to shake. "I don't understand."

"Liar!" She knocked him to the ground.

The cats moved closer, tails twitching, claws ready.

"Help!" he screamed. "Somebody, help me!"

~ * ~

"Hey." Tom, Anna's cameraman turned from his cell phone, somehow managing to keep the van on the road. "There's a disturbance at the museum. We're close. Want to cover it?"

Anna sighed and patted her graying hair into place. "What, some kid spilled a drink on an exhibit?" Hardly newsworthy.

"No. A guard was attacked and possibly killed."

She jerked up in her seat. "Let's go before Mr. Favored gets there."

"You bet." Tom whirled the wheel and they made a sharp U turn, barreling back down the narrow road.

"Watch it!" she shouted and then bit her lip. Tom had never caused them to have wreck. Yet.

A few minutes later they pulled into the parking lot and he shoved the van into a spot near the front door. He grabbed the camera while she opened her door.

Dashing to the entrance they pushed past museum security and managed to get all the way to the escalators before they were stopped by the police.

"I'm Anna Hershey," she identified herself to the young man in uniform, shoving her ID into his face. "Denver News."

"Yes, ma'am," he policeman politely answered. "I know who you are.'

"Then let me past."

"Sorry, can't do that. It's sealed off."

No doubt to preserve evidence Anna figured. Still, it was big news. She smiled sweetly. "Mind if we do a few background shots here while we wait?"

"Not at all." He turned to stop the next reporter.

She stepped to the side. The large overhead windows bathed part the dark hallway in light. She motioned to Tom to start filming.

"Good afternoon, this is Anna Hershey at the Denver Museum…." She went on giving the general background while her watchful eyes kept track of what was going on. The coroner had just gone up, along with a homicide detective. "That's a wrap for now."

Tom nodded and shut the camera off. "So now we wait?"

"We wait."

~ * ~

Her sandaled feet quietly padded into the Cairo Museum of Antiquities. Bast had left her faithful wreaking havoc among the farms in the land surrounded by water. The humans deserved their fate after crushing her children and using them to enrich the soil to feed themselves. Such desecration could not be tolerated.

She'd shifted back into her cat form. Her tail slowly twitched. She relaxed, yet kept careful watch. Above her sleek head lay the ruins of those from long ago, their bodies wrapped in dark brown and their faces long since gone.

"What are you doing in here?" She was asked in a tongue descended from the one she'd heard in ancient times.

Turning her head she looked back at the speaker, a woman dressed as they did today in soft colorful cottons. She heard the catch of breath.

"No. You can't be."

Ah, but I am.

~ * ~

"There's havoc everywhere," the man with a British accent said. "Dead bodies are being reported on various farms and witnesses swear the soil has turned to sand. Wheat crops are ruined and the prediction of high bread prices is causing a panic. People are rushing to the stores to buy what they can."

He paused, his usually impeccable suit looking as if he'd just thrown it on. "One witness reported seeing an Egyptian woman with what she claims was a cat's head, standing in the middle of the attack on her husband." He laughed nervously.

"Parliament is urging caution and the Prime Minister will be making a statement later today. In the meantime, it is suggested to owners to keep all cats confined until we discover if this is some type of virus spreading among the feline population, or some odd mutation we have no way to detecting.

I repeat, please don't do anything drastic until we have more information."

~ * ~

"Two guards dead," detective O'Hare said as he scribbled notes. He was one of those old-fashioned New York cops who didn't keep everything on this cell phone. Didn't much like the gadgets since information could easily get lost.

"Witnesses say," his partner Pat began.

The older man shook his head. In all his years on the force, he'd never heard such nonsense. "I don't buy a couple of mummy cats attacked the men and killed them. Looks more like maybe one of them wild cats got lose from the zoo."

"I called them, sir. They say nothing has escaped."

"Call 'em again. They'd have plenty of reasons to lie."

"Yes, sir." Pat dialed the number on his cell and took a few steps away.

"Damndest thing," O'Hare murmured, kneeling down to look at the body again. The coroner shifted restlessly on the sidelines. "You can take them now," he told the other man moving away.

Pat shook his head. "They say none of their cats are missing." He rejoined his partner.

O'Hare pursed his lips. "Might be true. Plenty of folks keep exotics even if they're illegal."

"Uh, detective," the corner interrupted. "You should look at this." In his tweezers was a type of brown wrapping.

Narrowing his eyes, O'Hare tried not to believe the evidence. Maybe the witnesses hadn't been lying or else it was most the elaborate charade anyone ever pulled.

~ * ~

Her city. Bubastis.

Softly she walked among the ruined columns, remembering their colorful displays. Her paws rejoiced at the feel of sand. Overhead Ra was falling once more into the realm of the dead to rise again from the fires in the morning.

At last, her path took her to the temple. Busted rock littered the once glorious place and painted eyes watched her approach.

"You've come home, my children," she praised. "You have had your vengeance upon those who desecrated your bodies and now you await your reward."

The meows from thousands of decayed throats greeted her news and rose above the once fertile valley. She bathed in their cries, happy to have brought her lost ones home.

"Behold, Anubis comes." She turned to face the echoing sound of large paws pounding upon the sand.

She did not have to see her people gather around her. Their excitement touched her very soul.

The jackal stopped a short distance away, bowing its head.

"We are ready," she said.

His canine form blurred into his human one, his jackal eyes watching her. With the ankh he held he motioned in the air and a yawning portal opened. Golden light escaped brightening the dead place.

"Come," she said, leading her people forward. "Now, we go to our reward."

~ * ~

"What do you mean all the cat mummies are gone?" Anna Hershey asked as she talked to curator at the Denver Museum on her phone. "Uh, huh." She listened making a few notes on paper. "All over the world? Yeah, I agree, that is strange. Thank you."

She hung up.

"Well?" her boss demanded, trying to look imposing.

"The killing has stopped." She sat back in the chair. It creaked slightly. "And there are some reports of strange lights coming from the ruins of Bubastis."

"Confirmed?"

She shrugged. "Hard to say. Most of the reports came from wandering merchants. My source in Cairo wasn't too sure about their reliability."

"What do you think?"

"I think someone went to elaborate lengths to pull a stunk." Her nails drummed on the desktop. "I'd sure like to meet the person who made this happen. They have several deaths to be held accountable for."

"But your story will be ready." Her boss wasn't questioning, just expectant.

"It will."

"Get to makeup. An hour before we broadcast."

"On my way."

~ * ~

Ra sailed along the river, his two fish swimming before him. Thousands of painted eyes watched, each tensing as if to catch his escorts and relaxing as he passed.

She bowed her head as the great sun god passed. It was her way of saying thank you. He raised a hand in acknowledgement and continued on his journey.

Sekhmet came to sit beside her. She stared up at the lioness.

"You did well," her larger cousin complimented.

"I did as I had to do."

"As was agreed."

As one the group began to move further into the underworld. Judgment for each awaited and afterward, she could go to live in the temple prepared and waiting for her.

Many of them would join her.

"I am envious," Sekhmet said. "I go to join the thousands of human warriors who fought in my name, yet you, will be allowed to dwell with your own kind."

"There will be some of your cousins. In the ancient times they were used in warfare."

"It will not be the same."

She understood and knew how truly fortunate she was.

At the appointed place the group stopped. Anubis took the heart of each, weighed it and sent the feline on to their reward.

She was last. He took her heart, nodded and pointed to the temple. "You have done well. Pass into your final dwelling."

Dignified, as was her station, Bast joined her people.

One way to pay it back in the writing community is to contribute to charity anthologies. Bast's Christmas Presents was written to help others. It's also when Seti finally revealed his name and that the worshippers of Bast smelled like Lotus blossoms.

Bast's Christmas Presents

Paws silent on the dirt path, the large cat paused, staring at the glittering lights adorning trees, bushes and anything else the humans had decided to cover. Dimly his ears heard soft talking and Seti wondered how a species who made so much noise could possibly survive. Cinnamon and chocolate laced the chilled air and assaulted his nose. The smell wasn't unpleasant, just annoying.

Snow drifted down trying to dampen his fur. If he'd been like his mortal ancestors, it would have bothered him and long since sent him to cover in a nice warm bed or a secure hollow. He no longer had need of those comforts.

Instead, he jumped off the wooden foot bridge onto the frozen water below. Lights lined the banks and he hurried down it, hoping no human eyes saw him. Granted, they might report seeing a Bobcat to those who ran the Chatfield Christmas Lights. During the day Seti had no doubt the rangers would search for him and find nothing.

Stopping on top of a snow-covered log, he listened and sniffed. Shades of blue and green bathed him. Further down the ice it sparkled yellow, red and purple. He supposed the humans found it beautiful. Seti thought it garish but he'd lived many centuries and understood the strange two-legged creatures had their own ideas on what beauty was. The painted pictures of his own people on the fading columns were proof of that.

He still remembered the family who had taken him in so long ago. They'd been honored he deigned to live among them, killing the rats who threatened the grain and their very lives. The place had been hot, with seasonal floods which brought life and a hardworking people who wore little. Some had even shaved their hair off and wore wigs instead.

Now, he was in a new land where seasons changed from hot to cold to comfortable in an irregular cycle. The people wore all manner of clothing as they did tonight. Most were heavily bundled in coats, hats, gloves and boots. Not that it was enough against the cold of the night. He figured most would stop at the warming hut about halfway through the light display.

He sat, his thin tail draped over his paws. Ears twitched, listening for sounds. Human voices he heard muted. He could hear them clearly when he chose, but now Seti listened for another sound. Bast had sent him here for a reason and he dared not disobey.

Finally, he heard what he sought. Faint mewling echoed down the frozen stream. Jumping down he followed the sound, pausing now again to tune out the loud laughing humans.

Near the end he had to pass under another wooden bridge. Humans stood on it, snapping pictures with their phones. He had no idea why they bothered since it was so dark. Surely the pictures couldn't be so good. Or were their memories so short they had no other way to remember the beautiful things in their lives?

Seti had no desire to find out. He had not lived with humans since Bast had released him from death and allowed him to walk the Earth as one of her Chosen Ones. Such a privilege came with a price. One he gladly accepted and had lived with for thousands of years.

The mewling grew louder.

His tail twitched and he waited until the humans finished snapping their pictures before he dashed under the bridge. He leaped off the ice back onto snow covered ground. He shook himself and rotated his ears forward to listen.

What he sought was close by.

Using the tree shadows and the dark unlighted places to hide himself, Seti approached the old historic white house. Lights shown through the windows and inside he saw shadows belonging to things of the past. There was a wired barn as well filled with ducks and geese who quaked and honked warnings as he passed them. They were rightful prey and they knew it. Lucky for them, he'd fed upon a plumb prairie dog earlier.

It would be amusing to stick around until spring when the body was found. There was a ranger who counted and numbered the dead. No doubt he'd be puzzled by an uneaten, decaying carcass, with a single wound upon its neck, completely drained of blood.

Not that humans believed in vampires and their disbelief protected the Chosen Ones.

Seti reached the second barn, its front open to the cold weather. Several tractors lined the final part of the path, each of them covered with lights and a huge sign asking the humans not to climb on them.

Passing under the fence he approached the line of trees each glittering in the dark. Red, white, yellow, blue and green beckoned those on the nearby highway to enter and enjoy the holiday light show.

Damp grass brushed his tawny sides and snow crunched quietly under his paws. No doubt the female would hear him coming. He expected a challenging hiss and growl. She'd think he was a danger to her and her kittens.

As expected, he came upon the nest. She'd taken over a rabbit den, already lined with leaves to insulate it from the cold. Two small kittens, one brown and the other white huddled against a thin female he thought far too young to bear them.

She hissed a warning, her tail flicking back and forth.

He sat at the entrance, not daring to enter. A female with kittens was dangerous. The worst she might do is fight him, at the very least run him off. However, this one was too weak.

"Bast sent me," he told her.

Her glaring yellow eyes bore into his brown ones. He noticed her short brown and white fur was matted and dirty. There were battle scars along her side and one toe from a back paw was missing.

No doubt she found him threatening because he was a male and his resplendent black spotted fur. He was also larger than even the Maine Coons with protecting black lines around his eyes.

"Why would the goddess send you?" she hissed back.

"You have heard of the Chosen Ones."

Her snarled reply answered him. "Get out."

"That, I can not do."

Not far away coyotes howled. Their yippy chorus echoed across the valley.

"You need food," he said, "or else you will not have enough milk for your young." He trotted away ignoring her indignant yowl.

Not far away was another rabbit hole and he dug at it, managing to kill the brown furred creature before it fled. He returned to the female's den and left the offering for her. She again hissed at him but didn't refuse the food.

He left her to eat and sat beside the entrance. A daring coyote darted toward him, thinking mistakenly, he would be an easy meal. It took only one swipe of Seti's paw to convince the canine fighting would be a mistake. It balefully glared at him while it retreated, a long gash along its snout.

After a time the human voices stopped and lights flickered out as the last of the cars pulled out of the muddy snow covered parking lot. The moon splashed light upon the white making the landscape brighter than it normally would be. Wind whispered through the skeleton trees producing a song more beautiful than those the humans liked to listen to. Somewhere in the distance a mountain lion growled and the faint chorus of wolves joined in.

Seti's ears twitched taking in the wildness of it all and rejoiced in the freedom he had. Bast rarely asked anything of him. For the most part he roamed and ate when he pleased, sometimes meeting another of his own kind. They shared their stories before continuing on the lonely life they preferred.

"Thank you for the meal," the female said.

He looked back at her. She had cleaned her fur and he could see what a true beauty she was.

"I am not here just to feed you. You need a home."

"I hate humans!" She shuddered. "You don't know what they did to me."

Actually, he did. Bast never sent him to rescue any cat without telling him the circumstances. "Bast told me."

"The goddess sticks her wet nose where it doesn't belong." Her tail twitched angrily. "Leave me and my kittens alone. We'll manage."

"I can't do that."

"I'll run you off!"

"I think not." He was patient with her. He could easily snap her neck. Bast would be furious if he did. Seti was there to help, not end the female's life.

"There is a place you can go," he began.

"I will NOT go to a shelter!"

He understood why. Although the humans tried to be kind,

the narrow boxes they put the cats in were cruel in another way. Not to mention always smelling one's own waste while trying to eat what little food they were given.

"There is a human who honors Bast."

"No human honors Bast," she spat back.

"That is not true." There were many who did. Bast knew who they were and often, as a Chosen One, he'd escorted an unfortunate cat to a worshipper's doorstep. "I have visited such many times."

"You would not lie to me." Did he hear a bit of hope in her tone?

"I would not dare Bast's wrath if I lied."

Her eyes darted to her den. "Will my kittens survive the cold journey?"

"It is not far." Bast would not risk the lives of two so young. "Would it not be good to not know hunger or cold again?"

She looked away. "It would."

"Then we have only to wait."

"Wait? We will not leave tonight?"

"No." He rose. "I will hunt for you again so you have food when it is light."

"Where will you den?"

"The rabbit you enjoyed will provide me with a place to sleep."

~ * ~

Every night humans came and went in their noisy cars, their voices carrying across the snow and fields. Seti watched them, waiting for the tug of Bast and the one who would rescue the female and her young.

He hunted regularly and kept away the coyotes both by leaving their muzzles scared and by spraying near his and her dens. Anything that came near fled in terror for the smell was so pungent. The female wrinkled her lips but made no complaint. It kept her kittens safe.

An entire moon cycle passed. Seti had just delivered a fat rat to the female when his head lifted. His ears heard the song of Bast and his nose detected the sweet flower scent attached to any who loved the goddess.

"It's time," he told the female.

She looked at the rat. He could see she was hungry.

"You have time to eat."

She devoured it quickly, taking the time to clean herself. Her kittens nosed her wanting to drink.

"Feed them," he told her.

"What if the worshiper of Bast leaves?" He heard her worry.

"The human will not." Bast planted an urge in the human. One they could not ignore and they would not leave until what the goddess wanted was found.

He exited the den and sniffed the crisp air. New snow covered the ground. Here and there tuffs of wilted grass poked out. Trees stretched their barren limbs toward the night hoping for the sun's warmth.

"I am ready." The female stood next to him, her two kittens tumbling over the snow. They raced back to their mother after encountering a blade of grass.

"Follow me." He led her across the valley toward the dangerous parking lot. Cars darted out unexpectedly and he had no desire for any of them of end up smashed under a deadly tire.

Retracing his path along the lighted trees, he ducked under the fence and behind the open barn. The one he sought was near. He sat in a dark corner, the female and her kittens close behind.

A group of three rounded the path, two men carrying cameras, one he sensed far older, and a woman in a long green coat. Her heavy boots make crunching sounds on the icy ground.

He couldn't see much else about the human female, but he knew the scent well. It reminded him of his past desert home.

"Cry out," he ordered his charge.

"What?"

"Cry out as if you're distressed."

The female hesitated before releasing a pitiful yowl.

He watched the human start. "Did you hear that?"

"Probably just a mountain lion," one of the human males replied.

"They don't sound like that and you know it," she snapped back. "We've heard them at the zoos. Besides, I doubt a cougar would be this close to a bunch of noisy people."

"You never know." He stopped and took a picture of the brightly lit house before joining the other male. Together they snapped more shots of the tractors.

"Here, kitty, kitty," the woman called.

"Go to her," Seti ordered.

"I don't trust her." She took a frightened step backward.

"She's a worshiper of Bast." He was growing impatient. The female only had one chance. If she failed to take it, both she and her young would perish.

The woman bent down and called softly, "Kitty, kitty. Don't be afraid. I won't hurt you."

"Go," Seti ordered again.

Hesitantly, the female stepped out, her head high and eyes searching for any danger. With each step she approached the outstretched gloved hand of the human woman. Slowly, the human removed the glove and extended her bare fingers. A sign of trust he hoped his charge recognized.

"Well, hello, there," the woman greeted as the female's nose tentatively sniffed the offered fingers.

The female darted back at an attempted pet, but the woman patiently waited.

"I know you're scared, but I can help you."

Both kittens darted out. The female whirled trying to stop them.

"Well, aren't you two cute." The woman allowed the pair to sniff her fingers. "Hey, Sweetheart, look at this!"

The younger of the two human males turned around and then slowly walked back to join his mate. He too knelt down, removed his glove and extended his hand.

A jolt went through Seti. Two worshipers of Bast! Their combined scent was overwhelming and he was heady with their fragrance. How fortunate this female and her kittens were!

"Too bad we don't have the carriers," the male said.

One of the kittens shivered.

"Oh, the poor things." The woman managed to scoop up the brown kitten and tucked it inside her coat. The female hissed in anger.

A second later the woman had also captured the white kitten.

Seti was pleased. "Let them catch you!" he ordered the female.

The human male made a grab and the female struggled a bit in his grasp. Then she went limp. The next thing Seti knew, she was tucked inside the male's coat.

"The last thing we need is another cat," the male said.

"We certainly can't let them stay out here. They'll freeze or else the coyotes we heard earlier will get them."

"Yeah, you're right."

"Besides," the woman rubbed against her mate. "You could pretend they're Christmas presents."

Amused and relieved, Seti watched the pair gather up their older male and the three left the holiday display. His assignment was done and he was beginning to get hungry.

The hot blood of a coyote beckoned.

In Missouri there is a wonderful cave that is easy to navigate. While visiting there, a sweet kitten decided he wanted to accompany us on the tour. His journey is described in Cave Hopes.

Cave Hopes

Baby cries from behind us.
Two round blue eyes plead
his small white furred feline body following,
tiny paws scraping on rusty earth.
He stops to explore an interesting crevice,
scrambling upward on the gradual incline,
looking down on us, crying for help.
I took pity on him, resting him between my twin mounds,
zipping him safe inside my blue fleece jacket.
His small body vibrates, his tiny purr loud,
slowly sinking, settling, secure,
stretched along the top of my black fanny pack,
napping through the long, damp cave tour,
missing the calcite and red iron soda straws,
the reverent voices of our admiration,
his warmth keeping away my chills.
He awakes at tours end as he's returned,
his hopes of a new home stolen.

Failure is both a cat vampire story and a traditional zombie mix loosely based on the practice of voodoo. Seti is in this story, as are the cat couple from Oasis.

Failure

The drums thrummed in his bones. Seti crept behind the tombstones, careful not to attract the attention of the priestess. Her followers wore bright clothing and danced around the blazing fire, oblivious to the cold and the falling snow. A table laden with foul smelling substances tickled his nose.

His ears detected the weak mewl of a kitten. Farthest from the fire, beside a tall tombstone its inscription faded, was a box. Three shapes huddled together and although he could not feel the freezing air, he had no doubt they did.

He hissed, his tail swishing back and forth. His eyes traveled back to the table now understanding why Bast had sent him. On it was the dead body of a cat, probably the mother of the discarded kittens.

"That one dares to walk in the realm of Bast," a soft voice said.

Seti turned his head. Beside him was a female, all black although he could see her spots beneath her fur. Female Chosen Ones were not common. Beside her was a male with coloring similar to his, tawny with black spots.

"It has been a long time," he greeted. He knew them both, Nesert and Hetep. They were not as old as him, but they both came from Pharaoh's land as did he.

"Bast sent us," Hetep said. Her yellow eyes darted to the box when a kitten mewled again. "That is my calling." She slipped into the shadows.

Nesert growled. "We are called to battle brother. For none except Bast is allowed to raise one of her own."

Seti knew it for truth. No doubt the spirit of the dead female had chosen to stay with the goddess. The priestess had no right to draw her unwillingly back to the land of living.

"How do we stop them?" Nesert looked to him for leadership.

"We keep their attention away from the kittens." Seti didn't yet have a plan.

"Hetep will need time to secret them away." Nesert sounded proud of her. Seti had heard rumors the two lived as if they were mated.

"Then we will give her that time and stop what this evil one has planned."

Seti could tell the drums were wilder now, the dancers acting as if they were in a trance. The priestess was chanting, her words crackling the air.

"Come." Seti bounded into the center of the dance, leaping wildly into the air and landing with a thump on the table. Several items rattled. Below him Nesert yowled, his voice breaking the spell. Several humans screamed and the drums stopped.

"What have we here?" The large woman leaned toward Seti. Her bright dress shimmered in the firelight. He could see her dark face and eyes. No doubt her hair was the same but she had a scarf wrapped around her head. Around her was a stench he knew well. He wrinkled his nose.

"You don't belong here." She made a motion with her hand as if to wipe him away.

Something like a weak wind passed him. Seti padded to the dead female and sniffed. Blood tickled his nose. Her throat had been cut, her blood drained. He could see its thickness in a silver bowl mixed with strong scented plants.

He arched his back, puffing up his fur. With little effort he released a piercing yowl. Many of the priestess' followers backed away. Some crossed themselves as if Seti were an evil they needed to be protected from.

"You a fierce thing. No scare me." The priestess began chanting again.

Nesert leapt up beside him. His added presence stopped the chanting.

"What is this?" She leaned close to them both and gasped. Her chubby fingers hesitantly crossed herself. "You both evil."

"She tries to control one of us, and she calls us evil?" Nesert's tone dripped contempt.

"She's testing her power." Seti wasn't sure how he knew this.

It was unusual for voodoo to be practiced in Colorado, let alone in a mountain town.

The dead female's legs twitched.

"She can't be allowed to call her back!" Nesert stepped forward, his claws out and battle ready.

Seti knew an anger he rarely felt or even allowed. If the priestess succeeded in making a cat zombie, then she would try next to fashion a human one. He'd heard of the evils caused by this magic.

The female's entire body convulsed. She tried to open her mouth but it was sewn shut. Seti saw the agony in her eyes and knew what he had to do.

"Protect her!" Seti ordered. He pounced on the human, his unexpected move forcing the woman to the ground. Clamping his mouth on her wrist, he bit her, drinking no blood. She wasn't rightful prey.

The human screamed, wrapping her other hand over her wrist. Scrambling away, she threw a terrified look at Seti. "Vampire!"

Her followers shrieked and ran. He heard car doors slam and gravel spewing. The priestess herself took one last look around and fled, her wrist dripping blood and leaving its stink on the ground.

Seti returned to the table and the struggling female. "I'm sorry. I was sent to stop this."

"We have failed Bast." Nesert lowered his head in shame.

"What of the kittens?" Seti asked.

The female raised her head, her eyes now reflecting concern and worry.

"I will find out." Nesert jumped down.

"There are three of us," Seti told her. "Hetep went to help them."

Her body relaxed, yet he could tell by her shudders she was in great pain.

Nesert returned. "There was a tent nearby. Hetep scented a follower of Bast and placed the kittens outside. She cried in distress and the human awoke."

Hetep joined them. She licked the muzzle of the female. "Your kittens are safe and under the protection of a worshiper of Bast."

"What do we do now?" Nesert asked.

Seti knew the female could not continue as she was. A Chosen

One yes, if that was her wish, but no cat should be forced to live as a zombie and under the control of another.

Popping and sizzling filled the air. The sounds distracted Seti and he looked toward the slowly dying fire. Out of its center walked a tawny colored female, jewels encasing her throat and glittering on her ears.

With awe he and his companions waited as Bast herself joined them. They all three lowered themselves, as was proper, their chins resting upon the table.

"I have failed you," Seti admitted, ashamed.

"This was not your doing," she answered. "Rather an evil human who sought power." Bast turned her attention to Hetep. "You did well. You found one of my worshippers."

Hetep blinked her eyes. "You honor me."

"You honor me."

"Nesert, you stood beside Seti in battle. You did well."

"But Bast," he began.

"You did well," she repeated. "Seti,"

He shivered when she spoke his name.

"You did well. I could not be more proud."

"But," he pointed his nose at the female.

"Seti, you did well. You stopped a far greater evil." She leaned down and touched the nose of the female. "I know it is your choice to be with me. I release your spirit to return to me."

The female's body completely relaxed and the eyes glazed over. Seti sensed her spirit had departed.

"Nesert, Hetep, go. You work is done. Seti, I have a final task for you. Make certain the body is burned." She leaped into the air and vanished.

"Until we meet again." Hetep touched Seti's nose. He faintly heard Nesert hiss.

"Go, as Bast said you should." In the distance he could hear a car engine.

Nesert and Hetep twitched their ears and jumped off the table. They vanished among the tombstones.

Seti grabbed the dead female by her neck and dragged her to the fire. He pushed her body into the flames and watched as it was consumed. The priestess would not be able to use it again.

Before he left, he'd make sure all the cats nearby, both those who lived with worshippers of Bast and those who didn't, knew not to be caught by the followers of the old evil. An evil he knew well although he had not battled it directly for many centuries.

Behind him were the sounds of those followers returning. He faded into the tombstone shadows. His ears heard the humans' desperate cries as they realized their plan had been ruined.

He lifted his head in pride. He had not failed Bast.

Illusion is the sequel to Failure and tells what happened to the kittens, who were once again threatened.

|llusíon

I think it wise we do not tell the humans of the Chosen Ones. Those who have gone to see Bast and then returned to walk the sands of Pharaoh. Even we do not speak of them. If we do, we watch with wary eyes because perhaps, just perhaps, one lurks in the shadows, listening.

Like the one who watches us now. Oh, he thinks I do not see him. His large form is not easily hidden behind the silly pumpkin my young human, Henry, carved last night. The rotten smell insults my nose. I honestly don't know why the holiday is celebrated with vegetables and costumes of ugly green nosed witches, skeletons, mummies, vampires and black cats.

Yet it is the last which concerns us the most. For once, when we died, we were wrapped reverently and allowed to pass to Bast. Ignorant humans stole us from the temples and used us to fertilize their crops. What an insult!

Vampires, my eyes again dart to the lurking figure. He had lifted a tan paw and licked it, using it to clean his ear. I could see the black spots scattered upon his tufted tan fur.

My litter mate crouched in fear behind me, terrified to be out tonight. His fur is black and already someone had tried to take him. They laughed talking of the pain they would inflect.

As for me, my fur is white and my eyes yellow. I am quite beautiful as a female should be.

"He has nothing to fear."

Had the Chosen One truly spoken to me? Why would he do so?

"You don't know human customs."

I remembered last Halloween the black cat several houses down had disappeared. His bones had been discovered during the warm time.

"I know them well." He left his hiding place and trotted up to me.

He was huge! I tried not to back away, but he frightened me. "Bast sent me."

Like his words meant anything.

"I am here to protect you both."

"I'm in no danger."

He cocked his head, staring at me as if I were an unknowing kitten. "There are more dangers than humans seeking sacrifice." He blinked. Were his eyes brown? "Look to the moon."

Moon? What moon? Where the bright orb would have hung in the night sky, I saw nothing except blackness and dim stars.

"Portals open. It comes."

"What comes?" A spot on my shoulder itched. I scratched it with my hind leg.

"Did your mother teach you nothing?"

"We were taken away when we were very small." Actually, our mother had died. We'd been fostered by a human with warm hands and who had feed us using squishy bottle nipples. I've heard it say we were fortunate to have lived at all. Our other brother had died.

"Ah." As if he understood something I did not. "You are the kittens who were taken to the worshipper of Bast."

I had no idea what he was talking about.

The Chosen One again looked to the sky. "Inside. Both of you."

My brother, coward that he is, scampered to our little door. He disappeared through it. As I went to go inside, the shadows seemed darker and to be creeping.

"Quickly!" I felt a paw against my back leg. I hissed and obeyed.

The Chosen One pushed himself inside. He sat next to our door. I watched as he extended his long claws and teeth. Teeth he used to draw life away from rightful prey.

"You have a place you feel safe?" he asked.

"We do."

"Then go to it."

My brother darted across the hard floor and heard him on the stairs. I knew I'd find him under Sara's, she raised us, bed. I started to follow.

"Go!" the Chosen One ordered again.

Instead, I turned back to watch. I sat in the doorway between what Sara called the mud room and kitchen. Coats hung on the wall, each person's boots lined up underneath. A basket bulging with toys sat there, along with our litter box. A stiff green rug that I hated because it hurt my paws sat inside our door. And coming in our door…

I blinked, not sure what my eyes showed me. Long ghastly white fingers stretched in our door, groping around, as if seeking something. The Chosen One lifted his claw and scratched the entire length of skin. Something howled. Not like a dog when the sirens blared. Its shrill shriek hurt my ears.

"Are your humans here?"

Now he asks. "No. They went to a party."

"Good."

The arm reached in again. He sank his sharp teeth into it. It screamed. Stepping back, he shook his head, dark, smelly blood dripping from his mouth. He spat it out.

Bushes rattled and a scampering sound went over the roof.

"Is it gone?" I asked, frightened, but not wanting to let the Chosen One know.

"For now."

"Why would it come after us?"

He didn't answer. Instead, he cleaned the blood away from his mouth and muzzle. When he finished, he looked at me. "You survived. It was not meant for you to."

I remembered Sara telling her friends how she'd found us in a box outside her tent. She'd been camping outside a small town in the Colorado Rockies. She'd searched for our mother and never found her.

"What happened to my mother?" I had to know.

"She dwells with Bast."

So he wasn't going to tell me. Had what happened to my mother been that terrible?

"It is better you do not know." His ears twitched.

"You're one of the ancient ones." I wasn't sure how I knew.

"The first."

Had I heard correctly? He truly had been the first Chosen One?

"I am Seti."

"My human calls me Celine. She named my brother Karp."

"Good names." He watched the door, his tail flipping. A faint dust whirled up.

Our house grew silent. Too silent. Even the dogs weren't barking and they always did.

"The evil is old."

"What evil?"

"It has been around since before humans and takes many forms. I have fought it most of my life."

"Why would it come for us?" I really didn't understand.

"Bast did not tell me."

I jumped back as the entire door rattled. Seti sprang into action, yowling and stretching his claws through the small opening. A loud thump, the sound of cracking, and the Chosen One darted outside.

Not able to stop myself, I dashed through to see the struggle for myself.

Outside he fought with a thing. Maybe it had been human once. Strips of cloth hung from a starved frame. The head had no eyes and two sharp fangs hung over what had once been a lip.

Seti held it by the neck. I have no idea why it didn't fling him off. After what seemed half the night, it stopped flopping around, its sightless sockets oozing.

"Is it dead?" Rankness filled my nose and I gagged.

"It already was." Seti cleaned himself before he forced me back inside. "First light will claim the corpse."

I didn't understand. "Was it the evil?"

"A servant of it."

Lights flashed in the window and heard the familiar whining engine. My humans were home.

"I will stand watch over it until it is gone. Go to your humans and stay with your brother."

He vanished out our door.

I greeted my humans who treated me and Karp to a few crunchy treats. They went through their usual routine of baths, reading a story and going to bed. Karp and I slept on Sara's, as we had since we first came here.

When morning came, I went to see if Seti was still there. He was gone. So was the dead thing. Only some dust remained on the grass.

Karp didn't leave the house all day. I sat in the flower garden and sunned myself. I found Seti sleeping in a dark corner, curled up under the urn Sara grows our catnip in. I left him alone.

After all, the Chosen Ones are not to be spoken of. The humans must never know. If they did, they'd hunt those like Seti down and do worse than kill them. He had proven to be much too fierce a warrior to have that unhappy fate.

Instead, humans must dwell in the illusion we are all simply cats.

Inspiration for Battle Companion came from a documentary about a famous film director searching for the location of Atlantis, which may be buried in an area off the coast of Spain. What if, from time to time, the city appeared, before returning to whatever fate had been decreed for it?

Battle Companion

We're known for our tempers and prized for our black pelts. Yet when the sun strikes my fur the spots are clear and in the night I can hide better than my orange cousins. The only unusual thing about me are my eyes. Most of my kind have yellow or gold ones. Mine are green, like the plants where I stand, my paw slightly raised, my nose testing the wind for any scent of prey or danger.

Not far away humans camped. I could smell their dank bodies and hear their muffled sounds. Light flickered among their tents, along with equipment I didn't understand and their death dealing machines. They hadn't seen me and I ignored them.

Long have I journeyed to reach this marsh. Nights away from the veldt of my birth and young life, through the many 'countries' as the human's call them, dodging their towns and other dangers they put in our paths. I heard their dogs bark as I passed and the hisses of their small cats who scurried into places so small I could not reach them. Not that I would have bothered them.

My destination was always clear and as I traveled I only hunted those who were rightful prey. I can not say when I first heard the call, but I have answered, and on this night where the moon hangs full in the star-studded sky, I can only wait.

How long I stood there I do not know or even when the prickling along my spine began. The shriveled grass began to dance and a shimmering sparkle wove patterns unknown to me. Slowly, from the sands rose high spires and deep canals emerged. Here and there places to cross without getting my paws wet. I could see figures moving among those strange buildings.

The call grew stronger and I could not ignore it. I padded to one of those crossing places and gingerly I placed a paw upon it. To my surprise it was solid and I crossed the water. A fish poked its head up to peer at me before swimming away with a flick of its tail.

I heard no screams from the humans on those smooth streets. They did not try to run from me, their hearts beating so fast I could hear them no matter where they went. Instead it was if I were expected. I did not understand, but keep moving forward, trying to find the source of the call that brought me here.

Further and further into this pearl like maze I went, until, finally, I stopped at the bottom of wide stairs. At the top stood tall pillars and between them a human female waited, her scent and dress reminding me of the ocean, damp and fishy. Her hair she'd pulled back and in her brown tresses a comb of seashells.

"I've been waiting," she said.

How I understood her I do not know. She did not speak in the snarls, growls or mewls of my kind.

I found myself at the top of those stairs at her sandaled feet. She knelt to place a cool hand on my head.

A sharp sound behind us and she looked away. I growled deep in my throat. I knew the sound. It brought death.

Their smell reached my nose first and I crouched, ready to spring, to bring death to them as they had my many cousins.

"You are safe here," the woman soothed. She faced those I had seen earlier in their tents. "You men are not welcome here."

"Are you crazy!" a man with a beard snarled. "This is the find of the century!"

"I would say you are not ready." A smile touched the woman's thin lips. "No doubt to you it would sound rather silly."

"We've been searching for this city." He raised his hands, the sweat staining his underarms. "And here it is!"

"A legend now proved." I turned my head to look up at the woman. "Yet you must leave here and forget what you saw." Her hand again touched my head. "We came for this one."

The man's shock registered on his wrinkled face. "A black leopard?" He laughed. "You're kidding right?"

"No." Her voice carried a quiet authority even I recognized. "To them was gifted a special intelligence."

"You mean a killing instinct."

"Yes and no. They fought beside us in war."

"The legends say nothing of war." He stepped forward, daring to place a foot upon the stairs "Much is lost in the mists of time's passing."

The tingling began along my spine again. My tail flicked uneasily.

"When we pass from this place, you will have no memory of us." The woman lightly stroked my head. "It will be as if you dreamed."

"I won't forget," the man vowed.

Again a smile upon her lips and I wondered how many times she'd heard such words in the past.

"Ah, but you will. We will remain a mystery unsolved."

"You were written of," the man began.

"By one who heard stories of us in a faraway land."

The buildings around us shimmered, fading before my eyes. I wondered if the humans below could see what was happening.

"What the..." the man stumbled backward, landing undignified on his rump.

"Farewell," the woman said, as the city sank beneath the sand and grasses, taking me with it into deep darkness.

When I opened my eyes again, I laid on something soft. The woman stroked my back. "You are safe."

I growled my fear.

"You are safe," she repeated.

I had no way to ask what I wanted to know. I growled at her.

"We travel," she explained, her fingers finding a spot behind my ear calming me. "We are indeed advanced as the ancient stories indicated."

Not knowing the stories I did not really understand what she was saying.

"My name is Katira. I am one of those who controls our traveling." She pointed to a smooth, round object sitting not far away. It hovered, not attached to a wall or a pillar.

Curiosity is something all of my kind share, no matter our size. I leaped down and tried to inspect the object. I raised my paw to touch it, encountering a stinging zap. I jumped back.

Behind me I heard her laugh. "It will not harm you."

I went to her, my eyes questioning and saw hers were the same green as mine.

"I have been waiting for you." She sank down and I put my

head into her lap. "You may not know the stories, but the ones like you remember your heritage."

Clanging outside growing closer. Thunder like a great storm echoed through the room followed by flashes of brilliant rainbow light.

Sadly she continued and her sorrow echoed inside me. "We have endlessly traveled in time and become a legend. Now, in the future, we fight for our survival." Her finger touched my ear. "I'm so sorry, dear one, to draw you into our conflict."

My heart quickened. Every instinct told me this was for what I'd been born. I rose to my paws, my tail whipping, my nostrils flared. The scent of blood filled the air. Rightful prey. Near.

Katira took her weapon, a blazing crystal sword, the handle encrusted with pearls. "You are my battle companion."

I knew her words to be correct and I was ready. Together we walked to the top of those stairs which first brought me to her. Below, in the red stained streets, the humans fought, others like me at their side, struggling against hairy, oddly clad creatures I did not know.

"Humanity lost to its primitive side," she sadly said, not moving to join the fight. Restlessly I stood beside her, ready to pounce. "We are all that remains of all which once was good." Her foot touched the first stair down. I willingly followed.

"Now, we must fight to preserve it against these…brutes."

My blood pounded.

"It has been a long, long fight." We reached the bottom. She raised her sword. I prepared to use my claws. "Now that you're here, the final battle begins."

My teeth sank into the leg of one of the creatures, its blood warm and right in my mouth. I ripped and tore, Katira ever at my side.

~ * ~

When the sun set, the dried marsh in which the city sat, glowed red and stank of death. The humans dragged back into the streets, their shouts of victory sounding like a shrill bird call only much, much louder.

Katira sank onto the stairs and I joined her. I washed the blood from my fur and my claws. Her hand touched my head. "You did well."

The seldom used purr rose. I rubbed my head against her.

"And you have earned your reward." Her lips touched my head and I felt an odd calm I had never known. My fierce temper gone.

She nodded as if all were as it should be. "Now, we rebuild the world." She got to her feet, raising her blood-stained sword over her head. "Today!" she yelled to her people and mine. "Together, we once again rise to our status as we were in the past." She smiled. "Long live Atlantis!"

Not sure where the idea for Intelligent Species came from, but its idea is intriguing.

Intelligent Species

We're more intelligent than you humans think. That's why the technicians hand one of us to you when you walk into the clinic. It isn't just to relax you like you're told. Sure, we're small and fuzzy, with cute faces, a tail, most of us have one anyway, there are few exceptions, and a pleasant purr. You like to scratch behind our ears or, for those of us who permit it, rub our tummies. We try not to use our claws when displeased. It ruins the mood.

Of course, the allergics all run shrieking and never come back. Good riddance. We don't like you anyway and hope the bad memory makes your life miserable. And even if you did find a place without us, the device doesn't actually work. The technicians just go through the motions of putting the pink or blue plastic bowl with all the colorful wires on your head and talk techno babble and twist the dials.

We're the ones who actually play in your minds. *We* find the nightmares, which keep you up at night or haunt you while you're awake. *We* help you get on with your lives and prosper and be happy.

But the public relations and marketing departments don't dare tell you that. If they did, well, you'd do the same things to us that those superstitious primitives did during the middle ages. We didn't like being accused of being evil familiars and being burned alive along with our chosen human.

This way is easier. We sit on your lap and purr while probing your mind.

Like the woman who is holding me now. She is thinking about some guy in her office she'd like to have sex with. What is this preoccupation humans have with that simple biological act anyway? It causes *way too many* of them to be born. I'll have to deal with that. Curbing the population is one of our goals.

And while I'm at it, I think I'll suggest she go to her local shelter and adopt a couple of us. She needs something useful to do with her time rather than think about men and how lonely she thinks she is. We'll make much better companions for her and sit on her lap while she watches her movies and eats her popcorn.

As for the memory she wanted erased, the silly one about the flub she made in the office a week ago, I think I'll leave that one. It'll make her think about her insignificant role there. It should force her to go out and find a better a job.

Because the more she makes, that's more of us she can adopt from shelters or maybe rescue off the streets. We *all* want a warm home, a soft bed, lots of attention, food and a servant human.

After all, did humans really think they were the most intelligent species on the planet?

The idea of an ice age has many possible outcomes, but what of the future generations who study what happened? The Storm asks that in a haunting way.

The Storm

Brooonnnggg, Brooonnnggg. The warning bells sounded over Nowhere, New Mexico and Mazie stuck her head out of the barn loft, glad she'd secured her long black hair in a ponytail. It kept it out her face while she worked.

"What in God's name," she began before her brown eyes widened. There in the distance and rapidly approaching was the reason. Even from where she stood she could see the whirling cloud of wind and snow. "Not again."

Mazie shuttered the loft and climbed down the ladder. Long ago she'd learned to wear jeans, a long-sleeved shirt and boots so she'd be comfortable doing her chores. She checked the cows and horses to make sure they had plenty of hay and water before tossing the last bucket of slop into the trough for the pigs. Grabbing her shawl she secured the barn door and rushed toward the house.

Brooonnnggg.

She just reached it as the storm blew onto her small farm. Her hands barely managed to open the door because the wind nearly tore it away. There was a brief battle to close it again as she fought her way inside to safety.

"Whew!" Mazie sagged against the plain wall listening to the ice pellets bombard her home as if she were an enemy it was trying to oust.

After a few moments she hurried over to the fireplace and tossed on a couple more logs. It crackled, the orange and red flames flickering happily, seeping warmth into her home and body.

Sooty, her dog, wagged his tail hopefully from where he lay on the hand braided rug. She never had been sure what breed he was with his thick black body, stumpy tail and a head that just looked too large sitting on his thin neck. His ears hung almost to the floor and his big chocolate eyes looked hopefully at her.

"Hi," she greeted, petting his smooth head. "At least you were smart and stayed inside by fire."

"Woofff," he replied in his deep baritone.

"Woof yourself." Mazie got up and checked on her dinner simmering on the wood stove. She's just added her new convenience a few months back when her crops came in and she'd traded several bushels of wheat and corn for it. Before that she'd cooked her meals in a pot over the fireplace.

The constant battering outside caused her to shiver. No doubt the storm would last for days. They often did.

"So much for global warming," she muttered under her breath remembering the lectures from school long ago. The politicians and scientists had been so worried about the planet warming up they'd been taken by surprise when the planetary weather patterns suddenly shifted. Great Britain, the Norwegian countries, most of Russia, Canada, and Alaska were buried under thick glaciers.

She'd heard New England and the mid-west were as well, along with most of the north western states. But no one had heard anything from them for several years so they didn't know for sure. Still most just assumed the worst. No news was bad news.

Her two-room home was beginning to warm. Mazie decided to push aside the quilt she hung over the door of her bedroom. Best to warm it up before night fell. Once darkness was upon them, the temperature would drop and she didn't want to bundle up and sleep next to Sooty by the fireplace. It just wasn't comfortable.

"Rrrrr."

She smiled at her cat. The little gray tabby was napping on the bed. "So sorry to disturb you, Bluebell." She'd named the cat for her brilliant blue eyes.

The feline got up, stretching, making the cat look longer than she really was. Mazie had found her under the barn one day as a kitten and had won the cat's trust over the short summer. Bluebell had moved into the house come fall and rarely ventured out.

"Like I'd make you go back and sleep in the barn," she chided Bluebell, running her hand down the cat's back. A rumbling purr rewarded her affection.

Going back into the main room, she again checked on her dinner. The smell of beef and vegetables filled the space making the place seem more friendly and normal, and not quite so lonely, despite the raging weather outside. She poured some into a cup, taking a sip. The thick stew warmed her insides.

She sat down in the only chair she owned, placing her dinner on the handmade end table, and tugged the afghan she'd kitted during the previous winter around her lap. Even with the combined heat of the fireplace and stove, the house tended to be chilly. Mazie picked up the book she'd been reading from the night before. She owned a few and at least the library had a decent collection from which she could browse, when the weather or her chores permitted the luxury.

Lost in the plot Mazie wasn't sure when she became aware of the difference in sound. Sooty growled deep in his throat and Bluebell crouched on the floor close by, the fur on her back spiked and her tail flicking rapidly.

There was a thunderous crack and her house shuddered. Bits of snow drifted down the flue causing the fire to hiss. Sooty released a mournful howl and Bluebell darted under her chair.

Mazie was on her feet looking around frantically. Her heart beat hard. Had the foundation broken or had part of roof been torn off by the wind? She did a quick inspection all around both the top and bottom of both rooms. Nothing seemed amiss.

"Oh, God, maybe the barn." She went to the door but didn't dare open it, not while the wind still blew. "Maybe tomorrow I can check." Not for the first time she briefly wished she'd married and not chosen to live alone.

"Too late now," she told herself. At the time, it had made sense because the only man who had wanted her was an older neighbor who really had only wanted her land and few animals. She'd loathed the man and had heard he'd beat his previous wife, who had run off. She had too much respect for herself and stayed single.

"It was the best choice." Yet, there were times, when it would be nice to have someone else around to help out and snuggle next to at night. She mused what would happen if she died and if anyone would ever find her body.

~ * ~

When morning came the storm still raged. Mazie groaned and forced herself out from under the pile of quilts she'd slept under. Both Sooty and Bluebell protested her moving. She grabbed her heaviest shawl, feeling her way across the bedroom and went to stoke up both fires. If it were possible, it seemed even colder.

"It wasn't like this last winter." There was no way she could check on the barn. Hopefully, if any damage had been done, the animals had found a safe place. If not, it wouldn't be the first time she'd lost livestock due to a storm. It was a fact of life living on a farm. Or so her parents, God rest their souls, had told her many times during her brief childhood before she'd had to take over running everything by herself.

Slowly the room began to warm and she made herself a light breakfast of oatmeal and toast. She had some tea left, a brew she concocted herself from various local plants, and the combination warmed her. She fed the dog and cat dried jerky and filled the water bowl from the hand primed pump.

"At least that hasn't frozen." It was one of the few modern touches she had. Most of the other farmers had to keep water in a milking can and refilled it from a central well.

There was shudder and she grabbed the edge of the dry sink. Sooty whined and Bluebell dashed once again under her chair.

"What is going on?" Mazie hadn't put a window in having learned from the examples of others what a bad idea it was. The winter winds were so vicious they destroyed many so no one built homes with any openings other than for a door and a fireplace chimney anymore.

The floor seemed to heave under her feet. She lost her balance and toppled to the floor. "Ouch!" Luckily, she'd landed on butt but she winced as she got back up. She rubbed the offended limb and then gasped. One wall of her house was now wretched up, giving the room a lopsided look.

"Earthquake," she muttered. It was the only explanation. And there'd probably be several aftershocks. Some parts of the country had them all the time. She couldn't remember though when there'd been one last in New Mexico.

"Really strange." She pulled her shawl closer and inspected the damage. There didn't seem to be any cracks. Mazie hoped there wasn't any, because if the wind got in…. She shut down her thoughts. She didn't want to go there.

With a backward glance at the wall she returned to her chair and picked up her book. The fire crackled and popped. Again tuck-

Bast's Chosen Ones and other Cat Adventures

ing the afghan around her legs she began to read trying to block out the constant ping ping against her roof. She noticed Sooty finally laid back down. He closed his eyes and fell asleep. Bluebell hissed at the offending wall before jumping up into Mazie's lap.

"I'm trying to read you silly cat."

As if that mattered. Bluebell kept pawing at her hand until she put down her book and spent time petting the cat. After several minutes the tabby changed her mind and jumped down, disappearing back into the bedroom.

"I should be used to her by now." With a laugh Mazie shook her head and went back to reading.

Long, long hours passed. She made herself a light lunch consisting of a beef sandwich and an apple. Afterward her eyes drooped and she fell asleep.

The next sound registering in her mind was a very loud bang. Her feet shook like the Earth had come alive. Sooty was howling so loud it hurt her ears and vaguely she could hear Bluebell yowling.

She tried to get up only to be slammed hard onto the floor. Black began raining down and she couldn't breathe. Mazie reached out her hands, trying to claw her way up, before the ceiling collapsed, shattering her back and forcing her into the final sleep.

~ * ~

"It used to be called Nowhere, New Mexico," the archeologist said as his student team joined him on the slight rise. The five turned their attention below, each heavily bundled up. They could see the church tower extending above a plain of white and black. "They had no warning. The old warning systems were gone."

"So why is it so important?" one of his students, Tim, asked.

The older man smiled, his gray hair hidden under his wool hood. "Because that's what we do. Unearth the past so we can learn about it."

"Don't we know all we need to?" his only female student, Laura inquired, shivering slightly despite her thick coat and boots. "According to the history books, Yellowstone went off and the blast zone was far more massive than was theorized."

"Yes," her professor answered, "we do know that." He fixed all of them with an authoritative stare. "What else do we know?"

Glen answered. "That it happened during one of the worst

~ 96 ~

blizzards during the early part of the ice age."

"And?"

"And," Henry continued, "the eruption lengthened it, causing it to last well into our time and for at least a couple of centuries beyond."

"Very good." The professor rubbed his gloved hands together. "Let's go down and take a look."

"We'll never be able to unearth it," Laura objected. "Not with the combined frozen ice and volcanic dust."

"Not this trip, no."

The group groaned as they carefully worked their way down the snow-covered slope and stood on top of the once thriving community. Under their feet, when they dared to peer down into the ice, were homes, and sometimes bodies of animals or people.

"Poor things." Laura wiped a tear from her face before it froze. To her right was the partial body of a woman. She tried to look somewhere else.

"Hey," Tim pointed. "What's that?"

They shaded their eyes as three figures approached, a pale woman wearing a nightdress covered only by a shawl, an odd-looking black dog and a gray cat!

"Hey!" Henry called.

The woman smiled and waved. "You found us," she shouted back gleefully.

"Not possible," the archeologist mumbled. "It's just not possible."

"How can we help?" Glen called.

"You already have," she called back, but it was like her voice came from a far distance.

"I don't understand."

Collectively they gasped as she vanished, along with the dog. The cat however, sat down, washed it paw and blinked bright blue eyes at them.

Dragons always travel with felines, or so the author learned. Danger said the Dragon is loosely connected to the Five Systems and the Borders universe and the second of the two stories using Atlantis.

Danger said the Dragon

Good thing I like to get wet.

I blinked my eyes and stared out at the falling rain. My short tail twitched and I glanced back at the com device. The message the Shellmaster had been waiting for had finally arrived. I would have to go tell him.

Placing my paw on the soaked, squishy ground, I padded my way through the ruins. Large chunks of wet, gray stone towered above me and instinctively I glanced upward. Predators could pounce down if I didn't watch for them.

Not that I'd seen any during the many sunrises we'd been here. The place was oddly silent. Oh, there were flutters I heard now again as chirping creatures flew overhead along with a slinking reptile whose narrow tracks I would see in the mud.

Otherwise, the Shellmaster and I were completely alone. I thought it odd considering the ruins we were investigating. Some intelligent beings had built them. Where they had gone or what had happened to force them to abandon their home, I had no clue.

I turned sharply and jumped up onto a narrow stone wall. I sat on my haunches, staring down below. In a hollowed out cleft the Shellmaster's long golden body quivered in excitement. His thin red tongue darted out between his long canines and retreated back into his cavernous mouth. His azure eyes darted up and he must have seen me because his short foreleg beckoned me to join him.

With great care I leaped down. My long legs had been made for running on vast savannahs, not rock climbing. I paused to lick at an offending spot on my paw before picking my way down the slippery path to join my companion.

"Most amazing," I heard him murmur in his odd draconian lisping dialect.

"They called," I rerowed back at him. My own voice is high and seldom used. Making noise scared away my food and then I went hungry.

His rectangular head bobbed up and down. It was a habit he'd gotten into since he often traveled with the Rovers. I guessed it made the humanoids more comfortable.

Shifting on his powerful hind legs, he angled his massive body so he could show me what he'd uncovered. I wondered how he managed to fit in the small space until I noticed how tightly his leathery wings were flattened to his scaled torso.

"Didn't you hear me?" I was annoyed he was ignoring my important news.

"Of course, of course." He used his snout to push some stone object out of its hiding spot and into the fading light. "Impressive, yes?"

Not so much but I knew I'd better humor him. "What is it?"

"No idea."

I saw the bunched hind muscles as he stepped out into the rain. I had to react quickly. With a powerful leap I managed to secure a place on the Shellmaster's back before he snagged the object in his back claws and launched into the air. Cold drops snaked along my short tan fur and I knew once we returned to camp, I'd spend a long time drying my black spotted body.

The flight was short and the Shellmaster dropped the object to the ground. There was a loud crack and a sharp hiss. My companion moaned as he landed. "Ruined."

"Maybe not." I slid down his damp body and landed easily on my feet. I sniffed and sneezed. The odor wasn't unpleasant. It was just—old.

"Ruined, ruined." He sneezed too as he examined the damage.

I viewed the crosswise fracture. The object was rectangular with writing scribbled on the lid and along the sides.

Using one back claw, the Shellmaster heaved the two pieces aside. He bent to examine the contents. "Odd."

"What?" I stepped closer to better view the interior.

"Should not be here."

I tilted my head to one side, my feline brain trying to decipher the puzzle. Packed inside was sweet smelling grass reminding me of my once vast home. Several scrolls were jumbled all through it.

"Egyptian," my dragon companion said.

From Egypt? How did they manage to find their way from Earth to Ariel?

"Great puzzle," he continued, his tongue darting out again and his body shivering. "Great puzzle."

He could have his puzzle. Right now I wanted to hunt. I darted off in search of a fluttering creature. They were small but tasty. When I returned, the stone box had been shifted inside our huge wer-silk tent, its contents carefully laid out on the fur covered ground.

I began the important task of cleaning my fur. Blood attracted the slithering thing and I had no desire to sample its bite. Also, I wanted to be dry.

As I settled down for my nap, I heard the Shellmaster humming to himself. My overly large ears twitched at the familiar lyrical draconic music and I allowed my eyes to drop shut.

I opened them in complete panic. There was nothing below me and I frantically clawed for some secure hold. My body tumbled before being tossed to one side by a wind so powerful I feared perhaps I'd been caught up in a turbulent cyclone. All motion stopped abruptly and I landed with a soft squish. I shook my limbs, daring to gaze around at my new surroundings.

A large bright moon sat in the dark night sky. Ariel had no moon. Clangs and shouting echoed across the plain. Tall grass swayed in the passing breeze and insects sang their distant song.

My body tensed, wanting to run, but I forced my mind to control my instincts. Was I alone in this strange place or had the Shellmaster also been brought?

Not far away there was a snarling hiss and the sound of something very heavy thrashing about. I headed for it, slinking through the grass as if I were trying to evade a predator.

"Bad."

I recognized the draconian word. Relieved I had not journeyed here alone, I pushed through the vegetation and found my companion. He shook himself gingerly testing his hind legs. His wings snapped as he unfurled them.

"Not injured."

"Good," I replied. "Now what?"

"No idea." He rose to his full height, checking out our surrounds. "There's a moon."

He'd noticed the difference as well.

"Come." He crouched down and I leaped to his back. His massive wings carried us through the sky. "Gravity similar."

"That good or bad?"

My companion didn't answer. Instead, he flew toward a dark mound in the distance. As it came closer my nose detected the familiar scent of humanoids along with other animals which my people had once known.

"Not Ariel," the Shellmaster said.

"Earth." It could be no where else.

"Agree."

We passed over some sort of high tower. Two men were there and I heard them shouting in a tongue unknown to me. One tossed a long object and the dragon banked to avoid its sharp sting.

As we passed over the city, I took the time to study its shape. It was almost circular, with strips of land squeezed between bands of water. One long river connected them all and along it swam wooden and papyrus boats.

"Not good," my companion muttered. I heard his worry. There were regulations we'd no doubt had broken, particularly regarding Earth.

He flapped his strong wings and carried us toward the distant mountain. On it sat a huge circular temple. One of the courtyards held steaming baths and a fountain spewed heat into the chilly night air.

"When?" my companion breathed, before floating up and soaring over the vast grassy plain. All types of animals ran as we passed overhead. Some were familiar to me, others completely unknown.

As dawn touched the sky, the Shellmaster folded his wings and dropped to a smooth landing. I jumped down and shook my body. Riding, although a long-established routine between us, wasn't bad but my legs tended to get stiff.

"Where are we?" I asked as I sniffed the air. I was hungry.

"Somewhere that should not be."

"And where is that?" There were times I tired of his cryptic comments.

"Ancient place. One of legend and myth."

His answer still didn't help. I wasn't one who studied the ancient texts and snooped around ruins. The Marllon dragons did. The Felcats kept the histories. But I wasn't one of them. I was descended from Servals and chosen companion of the Shellmaster.

I twitched my tail. Not far away rightful prey skulked. "I'm hungry," I said and vanished into the thick underbrush. Sinking to my belly I watched several thick furred creatures nibbling the grass. They lifted up, sniffed the air and sank back down to eat.

I waited until one dared to hop away from the others. My eyes watched it as my behind wiggled just as I pounced. A high-pitched squeal pierced the air as I broke its neck. I heard the others scuttle away. I devoured my meager meal, cleaned the brackish blood from my short fur and rejoined the Shellmaster.

He'd found a cave and had probably decided it was a good place to inhabit. Debris rolled out the entrance partially hidden by a large black rock. I waited until nothing more exited before rejoining my companion.

Water dripped into a small pond near the back of the dragon sized cave. It was cool but not unpleasant to one such as myself. The Shellmaster turned his head to look at me. "Welcome."

"You made a good choice," I approved.

"Me think so." He lowered his mass to the uneven stone ground, relaxing his wings so they spread out around him.

I'd often sheltered under those wings when we'd camped at various sites. Predators instinctively knew he was more dangerous than they so I never worried about being attacked.

I blinked and padded across to drink the water. It was sweet with a hint of wildflowers. My tongue cleaned the last of the moisture away from my mouth. "What now?"

"Sleep." His eyes dropped closed.

Rustling alerted my ears and hoots drifted through the night. From somewhere a scream of rightfully downed prey echoed and the victorious howl of the hunter. I laid down next to musty smelling draconic body and slept, although a part of me always stayed alert.

When morning dawned, I stretched, my long back enjoying the sensation. Again I drank the flowery water and bounced to the entrance. The sun slowly bathed the land around me, the shadows shifting to recognizable shapes. Towering green leafed trees spread their branches over the tall yellowish grass which shivered in the morning breeze.

My ears twitched and part of me longed to run and run until my legs tired. I felt I had come home.

"You are home." I looked back at the Shellmaster.

"Not really. I only know of Earth through the stories my mother told me."

"True. Your kind, long companions to us."

"Not us only." The shellmasters traveled with a variety of feline companions.

"Agreed." The dragon awkwardly shambled over to join me. "Question be, when on Earth?"

A hint of sulfur bite my nose and I rubbed at the annoyance. "Stink."

Rumbling shuddered under my paws and I saw the Shellmaster yank up in distress.

"Not good. Not good."

"We're in danger?" Instinct dictated I run yet my intelligence said to stay put.

"Not know." He sniffed. "Time to hunt."

"Each of us our own way." I didn't feel like a ride today.

"See soon."

I jumped outside and darted off toward the trees. Overhead the dragon's shadow passed and I heard the alarmed screeches of various inhabitants. It made it harder for me to hunt but I found an injured brightly colored winged creature.

After my meal and rightful bath, I returned to the cave. The Shellmaster stood outside, his attention riveted on a group of travelers below our perch.

Several lightly clad humans were in the clearing, their smell easily detectable to the prey they no doubt sought. I guessed their intention from the various odd implements they carried. I'd read some and identified some lances plus bows. Their sounds drifted up the narrow canyon and I could see them gesturing.

"Bad hunters," I said.

"The box!" The Shellmaster lifted up on his hind legs.

"What?"

"There!" He awkwardly pointed.

I looked again and saw a bright colored container sitting on the back of a wagon. "Are you sure?" What we had found had been dull and some of the writing unreadable.

"Yes." His tail moved side to side. It did that when he got excited. It made him more feline.

A rumbling shook the mountain and rocks loosened, skittering and hopping down the narrow canyon. The humans shouted and brown horses reared up. I didn't know if they could control the fear filled animals.

"Come."

He bunched his hind quarters and I instinctively jumped to his back. I wasn't sure what he intended to do. Before I could ask, my companion was in the blue sky, circling down to the humans.

"No," I huffed.

Several of them ran away, yelling. A couple stayed, both of them dark skinned, adorned in sheer white, their eyes encircled with black similar to mine, and adorned in gold, blue and red hanging around their necks, middles and upper arms.

One raised a spear. The other raised his hand as if to stop the attack. His black eyes watched us.

The Shellmaster landed near the wagon. I could smell the fear of the horses yet they didn't run.

"What are you doing?" I asked.

"Box." He leaned down to examine it.

Warily I watched the humans. I tensed, ready to strike if I sensed any danger. Humans were weak creatures and their necks broke easily. Or so I'd been told by my mother.

The human who had raised his hand spoke. I didn't understand the words.

My companion lifted his head, his tongue darting out. It touched the ground, tracing several figures.

I heard the human gasp. He climbed out of the wagon and came to see what the Shellmaster had written.

"What are you doing?"

"Want to know when/where we are."

I thought he understood we were on Earth and probably in the past, since I had not seen nor heard any spaceships.

The human thrust out his arm and I heard the sharp tone. A lance was given to him. He made symbols with it.

"No!" the Shellmaster hissed.

"What is it?"

He didn't answer. Instead, he made more markings on the ground. The human read them and shouted at the other.

"What did you tell him?"

"He need to leave. Quickly."

"Why?"

"Danger." With a final wistful glance at the box, the Shellmaster launched into the sky.

I hung on tight. "I thought the box was important."

My companion didn't answer. Instead, he soared in the blueness. He followed the humans back to odd circular city, staying until he was satisfied they were safely on a papyrus boat and out into the vast water.

"I don't understand." My legs were getting stiff. I needed to dismount and walk.

"We're…" he began just as the smoking mountain reached up trying to swallow us in blackness. I felt its hot breath and smelled its sulfur stench. It spat a large burning rock and the Shellmaster barely dodged it.

I dug my claws into his scaled flesh. I hoped I didn't damage my companion's back.

He folded his wings and dived down, but the lower we went, the thicker the darkness.

My ears barely detected the screaming humans. We skimmed over the city before the dragon changed course and away to what I hoped would be safety.

The mountain exploded behind us, the sound bouncing us and I feared my draconic friend would plunge into the deep water.

He matched speed with the fleeing papyrus boat, keeping just behind it.

A roaring reached my ears. I dared to turn my head and I saw the rising water pursuing us, almost faster than the Shellmaster could fly.

"We're in danger!" I yowled.

Just as the menacing wave would have knocked us from the sky, the Shellmaster dropped down, his wings protectively surrounding the boat.

I howled in protest just as the water covered us and sputtered the liquid out of my sensitive nose. Then I was back in the sky, shaking my body and wishing I dared to dry my fur.

"They're safe," I heard the Shellmaster say.

The boat bobbed in the water. Many of the humans were crying while others manned the oars. Several times the high waves came and each time the Shellmaster protected them.

I'm not sure how I stayed on his back. Many times I felt as if I was about to be ripped away and dug my claws in further.

When the shoreline finally appeared, the boat slipped between two giant rocks and glided into the rippling waters of an inland sea. My companion landed on the top of one of the spires.

One of the humans waved.

The Shellmaster rumbled his response.

We stayed there until they vanished from sight. I took the time to dry my fur enjoying the hot sun on my back.

The punctures I caused healed rapidly. It was a gift the dracos had.

"So," I prompted when I finished. "Just where or when were we?"

"Atlantis."

I blinked my eyes as my mind digested what he said. The city was myth. Or so I'd always believed.

"Why did we protect that ship?"

"The box." He extended his wings to dry them. "Legend says," his sides quivered in excitement. "Golden dragon tell Egyptian of danger."

It did?

"Now. We find place."

He shoved with his hind legs and once again we flew. Where I supposed it didn't matter. Maybe we could go find the sprawling land of my ancestors. There would be good hunting.

I suggested the destination to the Shellmaster. He agreed and dropped down to the calm sea. Water sloshed over his back and sprayed me.

It's a good thing I like getting wet.

More Lives blends the cat vampire stories plus the events in my two books God's Gift and Winter Awakening. In the latter, journal entries are discovered written by a little girl who suffered an unknown fate. This story reveals what happened.

More Lives

Amentet lifted her paw from the cold freezing ground and sniffed with her gray nose. Not far away rightful prey shivered in its den causing her hunger to increase. The night before she'd not eaten because the deep snows kept her confined in the abandoned house where she'd taken refuge. Not that she'd minded sharing it with the frozen human bodies. She'd just wished there had been some mice. They too it seemed had fled to the warmer south.

Wind fluttered through the white skeletal Aspen trees. The groves they grew in peppered the mountain side. Slowly she descended down the incline, noting how the deer were stripping the bark, leaving hanging strips. Vaguely it reminded her of the cloth the priests had used to wrap the mummies for burial.

She paused occasionally to track the scent of the long ear, or a jack rabbit, as the humans called them. It was near death and she needed to hurry. The blood was bitter if it died first.

Sinking on her belly, she slithered through the brittle grass. The long ear was in a hollow under the huge pine tree. She heard its heart flutter, preparing for the final beats before the cold claimed it. Raising her hind end, she made the short dash and was on her prey before it died. Warm sweet blood filled her mouth and filled her body.

When she finished, she washed herself, as was proper, and left the carcass to rot. Trotting to the entrance, she gazed out upon a land devastated by volcanic ash and now a cold, long winter. Moonlight barely shone through the heavy gray clouds and thick wet snow covered the landscape.

Not far away she could see a frozen fawn at the bottom of a rocky ravine. It had probably been left there by its mother who, for some reason, had never returned. Not far away the empty husk of a snake crackled as the wind rolled its pieces over the edge. A wolf howled, answered by the rest of its pack, their chorus a welcome relief to the death now shrouding the forest.

Her thin tail slowly moved back and forth. She had time to reach the human town she saw in the distance before the sun weakly shone upon it. Her ears twitched as the wolves continued to sing. They hadn't scented her, so she should be safe.

Stepping once more out into the cold, she marveled how Bast's gift kept her from feeling the freezing bite. True, she had died a rightful death. A Roman chariot had smashed her first body under its heavy metal wheel. She hadn't even heard the laments of her human family and vaguely wondered if the one who had killed her had been put to death as per Egyptian law.

Instead, she had opened her eyes and found herself upon a soft golden pillow resting at the base of temple stairs. She'd climbed them, amazed at the humans who guarded it. Their thin white robes fluttered in the lotus flowered breeze. Passing the columned entrance she'd found the marble floors covered with cats.

In the center sat Bast, her sliver, black spotted, fur glistening from fastidious cleaning. Proudly she sat upon piled pillows, several kittens daring to pay with the goddess' tail. Her green eyes watched Amentet intently as if something of great importance was about to happen.

"Welcome," Bast had purred her greeting.

She'd sunk to her belly. It was the proper way to greet a goddess.

"There is no need. All are equal and welcome here."

Amentet's green eyes had darted to the side. Several large males lined the stone wall. Their fur was tawny, with the same black spots as Bast. Their normally green eyes glowed an eerie red.

"They are my Chosen Ones," the goddess had said.

"Chosen Ones?" A shiver had run through her body. Dark were the whispers and tales she'd heard of them.

"They are nothing to fear." Slowly the goddess had risen to her paws and approached Amentet. "Often I have chosen males." Her warm nose had touched her gray one. "But in you I sense..." the goddess had not finished.

Backing away, Amentet had known a moment of pure fear. Was she to be condemned and sent away from what was her rightful award?

"Never!" Bast had vowed. "I offer instead a choice. You can live but your one life. Or," she'd trotted away and reclaimed her place on her pillows. "I offer you eight more."

"How can this be?" Amentet was curious, despite her fears.

"Become a Chosen One."

Again her eyes darted to the males. Some cleaned dirty spots on their fur, others watched her. Some had been more interested in the colorful birds fluttering overhead.

"It is my choice?"

"Always." The goddess had lifted a silver paw and pulled at her claws.

How long Amentet had considered the choice, she had no clear memory. In the end, the males had all left, she supposed to wander the Earth. The other cats had left as well. She'd been left alone with the goddess.

The decision had come quickly and Amentet consented before she changed her mind. "I agree."

"So be it." Bast had again approached her and touched her nose. "Go in peace, Amentet."

When next Amentet awoke, she found herself ripping out of constricting mummy wrapping. She poked her silver head above the suffocating desert sands and blinked in the bright sunlight. Ruins littered all she could see. There was no evidence of her beloved family or any other human either.

Pulling her thin body out of the sand and she sniffed the dry air. The heat beat down but it had no effect upon her. She had no desire to find a shady, cool spot and sleep. Instead, she pounced upon a rat, drained it and began her journey across the desert.

During her wandering time she sometimes met another of the Chosen Ones. They would hunt together for a few nights and then part company. Amentet found it odd that of all the females she'd been selected, yet the oldest of them Seti, assured her she was not the only one.

"There are other females," he'd told her. "You might encounter them. Or you might not. It is difficult to know."

Sliding down a snowbank and pulling her thoughts away from the distant past, Amentet stood at the edge of a frozen lake. Houses and other buildings were bunched at the far end of the narrow valley.

Across from her stood several small buildings and she could tell from the stench, it contained human waste.

A small figured wrapped in a thick brown blanket struggled against the strong wind. She knew it was child. It stumbled up the embankment and collapsed, shaking violently.

Although she had not craved human companionship, her heart softened and she gingerly stepped out on the ice. Even as a Chosen One she didn't like the feeling of getting drenched. There was no cracking and she hurried as fast as she dared to the other side.

"Rerow," she greeted the child.

"Kitty," the child responded, putting out a hand.

She sniffed the fingers and knew the scent of a female close to death. Why ever would the girl's parents allow the child to be out here alone and freezing?

A shudder shook the girl's body. Amentet wished she had warmth to offer. Perhaps she could help in another way. She nipped a finger hoping to urge the suffering youngster to her frozen feet.

"Ouch!" The child frowned. "Bad kitty!"

You must get up! She knew her thoughts would not penetrate the girl's mind.

"Cold." The little girl wrapped the blanket tighter around her shaking body and struggled to get up. Her feet slipped several times in the snow until she finally got to her hands and knees. Slowly, she crawled up the hill to the smelly bathrooms.

Amentet followed, ready to nip an ankle if the child stopped.

Instinct must have guided the child because the girl pushed the heavy door open and staggered inside. Amentet slid in beside her.

"Stinks," the child said as she slid to the chilled floor and shook violently.

Amentet agreed but at least the youngster was out of the storm. Snow dripped from the girl's head and puddled beside her on the concrete floor.

Wind shook the structure causing the metal roof to creak and rattle. It forced the door open and it stuck open, invading the small room with freezing damp air.

"Burr." The child tried to wrap her blanket tighter around her cold body. She'd stopped shivering and Amentet knew death hovered near by.

Taking pity on the child, Amentet crawled into the girl's lap.

Frozen fingers touched her short fur and she heard mumbling noises escape the cracked blue lips.

Soon, the fingers stopped and the child fell asleep. Amentet sensed the breathing slow. She lifted her head and watched–the silent guardian of the dying girl.

A haze began to form beside the girl's cooling body, solidifying into a human man. He wore a long red robe of a style from another era, with hair the color of night. He put out a scared hand and took the hand of the child as her spirit emerged.

She smiled at him and he swept her up into his arms. "Your parents are waiting for you."

His kind brown eyes looked down at Amentet and his skin reminded her of the desert people she had once lived with. She was glad he had come to escort the child into the afterlife.

"You are welcome to come as well, Amentet," he offered.

Beyond him she saw the golden gate to a place she had heard of in her travels. It was a new belief replacing those of the ancient land from whence she'd come.

Getting to her paws, she jumped off the now dead body, and flicked her tail. Part of her wanted to accept. Part of her did not.

He must have sensed her decision before she did for he smiled at her sadly.

"My thanks," she told him. "But I have eight more lives to live."

In the future beyond the Winter trilogy, cats are hunted and killed because of their intelligence. My Mother's Stories provides a hint of what happened after the ice melted and what type of human society developed.

My Mother's Stories

Normally, I'm not afraid of heights. My kind are used to climbing rock cliffs and staring down upon the world. But I know should I slip and fall, those white fluffy things below would not be soft. Instead, I would plummet through them and meet the goddess in a most undignified way.

I jumped down, removing my paws from their precarious perch upon the wooden railing. The hissing of the engines and the shouts of the humans who kept them running reached my ears. They were taking a huge risk protecting us. If caught, the Lords would banish them to the far west, a land long dead and buried under tons of black.

My green eyes drifted above noting the huge sail fluttering in what little breeze existed at this height. The sky above it a clear blue unlike the ugly brown most saw on the ground. Even further above I saw the deeper navy and knew eventually they faded into black and airlessness.

Part of me still wondered why not all felines had followed Moon through the portal. My mother had told me the story before she had been found by a Lord and killed. I shuddered at the memory. Most humans feared us. They claimed to be the only intelligent species upon this world, ignoring all others and putting us to death.

Clunking boots upon the stairs brought my attention back to the ship's deck. The *Capture*'s captain stood there, his feet braced against the slight sway, his broad shoulders back, his nostrils flared as if he tested the wind's scent. His brown eyes darted to me and I noted the crinkles around the edges.

"So, Climber, where next should we search?"

Captain Reynolds Umbra dedicated himself to saving other

intelligent species. The gash upon his face he'd received from a Lord's sword. He'd never told me the entire tale, but I knew he wore it with pride, having seen him start many a fight over it.

I couldn't really answer him. Writing was beyond my ability since my paws are not designed to clench a quill.

"Perhaps to the far west." I heard his wistful tone. He marched over to the railing and looked over the skies. "There aren't many of us who have mastered the skies. At least this is the one place the Lords can't follow."

The Lords and Scholars had made the use of any type of technology a flailing offense. I'd seen the results in many markets, when I dared to leave the ship. The common folk skirted the mutilated bodies being devoured by insects and birds.

"Granted it might mean we'd run low on supplies." His rough hand scratched his bearded chin. Long red hair cascaded down his back tied back by a leather throng.

Supplies were a human concern. I had plenty of prey in the lower decks. The wily rats seemed to always be present, no matter how many I hunted and ate.

"Might be safer though, considering Lord Harrot has decided to hunt me."

Lord Harrot inhabited the largest tower. It perched like a hawk on a huge cliff, the water crashing on rocks below. I'd heard he'd decorated it with many relics, some of which I suspected were illegal. After all, there were some freedoms the Lords allowed themselves that others would be punished for.

Fingers stroked the back of my head and I allowed the privilege. I leaned against the human flesh enjoying the rare attention. Rumbling started inside of me and I did not stop it.

Reynolds laughed. "Like that do you?"

I blinked in response and then hissed. Not far away another sky ship bobbed above the clouds. Even from this distance I could see the broken mast and the red-orange flames slithering along the upper deck.

The captain bellowed, "Heave to!"

The crew spilled onto the deck. Reynolds raced for the wheel. Slowly our vessel turned and headed toward the ship in distress. Shadows began to form along the deck and my fur bristled when I realized who there were. I had no way to warn Captain Umbra.

Closer and closer we sailed. I hunched down and hissed, my thick furred tail slapping from side to side as I readied for battle.

Boom!

Wood splintered and broke. They missed our mast, but hit the side railing. Two humans fell overboard, their screams muffed by the second canon shot. I said a quick prayer to Bast and scrambled from my perch just as the mast fell, snapping more railing.

What followed next was complete mayhem. The Shadows swung onto the *Capture*, swords swinging. Gurgle sounds escaped the crew's throats. I scratched several ankles and felt a blade pierce my back. Warmth trickled through my fur. I ignored it.

I didn't see the net until it was too late. I tried to escape. It ensnared me, keeping me from running. I flopped on the deck, hissing, snarling, trying to use my claws to rip myself free.

All too soon the fighting stopped. The Shadows lined the few survivors up and tossed me at the feet of my friend. "I'm sorry," he said, before his expression hardened.

"Hello, Captain."

Even I knew the gravelly voice of Lord Harrot. "How good to see you again."

Reynolds spit blood upon the deck. That earned him a slap.

"You'll be respectful."

The captain laughed.

"I see you still have—that." I couldn't avoid the foot. My head snapped back and I yowled in pain.

"Stop that you devil!" Reynolds sprang at the Lord. Black gloved hands held him back.

"Still have fight in you, eh?" The Lord chuckled. "Put this abomination on the ground."

I sensed the loss of altitude and felt a jarring that hurt my entire body. The *Capture* groaned as if it were alive and pitched onto its side. I slide, as did the captain. He managed to keep me from smacking into the side.

"Easy, Climber." His finger gently touched my head. "I'm so sorry what has been done to ye."

Shadows surrounded us, forcing the humans to their feet and out onto a thick ebony. The captain carried me. I longed to be out of the net.

"I'll give you a ten count to run," the Lord drawled. "After that, well–" He pointed to the line of dark shapes. "They can do with you what they will." He took the reins of the well-groomed horse awaiting him. "Even if you escape, you won't survive."

"Well," Reynolds muttered, as if amused. "I said I wanted to see the far west."

Harrot began to count. "One, two, three,"

Umbra ran, holding me against his chest. If he were struck in the back I'd be squashed. I kept hoping for an honorable death, yet it seemed the goddess would not grant me that one small favor. I wondered what I had done to offend her.

"Five, six,"

A blade appeared and suddenly I was free.

"Run." My friend paused, putting me on the ground. "Run!"

"Eight, nine,"

I ran. I dared not look back, even as I heard the cries of the crew as they fell. The victorious whoops of the attackers echoed over the dead land.

I ran.

Dark fell before I stopped. As I tried to breathe through the pain, I saw in the distance blue-white flames. Pops and sizzles echoed and vaguely I saw Shadows dancing. I knew none of the humans I traveled with had survived. The dark ones who raided the sky left none. Why a Lord had used them to accomplish his goals…

I just hoped Bast wrecked her vengeance upon him.

I found a small hollow and licked my wound. My ears twitched and the eerie silence haunted me. No birds sang. No insects buzzed. No rats squeaked. Long had I heard of the far west and the damage left by a vengeful god. Or so were the whispers I'd heard on the few occasions the captain had dared to visit the city.

The Scholars and Lords taught humans had been mercifully spared. So was it ordained they be the rulers. All others had to be put to the sword. It was their god's will.

It was why they hunted the few remaining intelligent cats.

I had heard other forbidden tales. Many humans had escaped on ships. Some to the south but others, for those few who dared admit it, to the stars. The latter was never mentioned. Publicly. If they were caught, they disappeared. Or worse. Why the two legs treated each other that way I couldn't understand.

True, we had our own mating battles, but we never killed. I

wondered then what had become of the last litter I had sired. Had they lived to become adults? Or had some human found them ending their young lives.

I turned my thoughts away from such sad things. Lowering my head to my paws, I dared to close my eyes and sleep. Every part of me hurt.

With the rising sun I opened my eyes. The brightness stabbed me. All I wanted to do was return to blessed sleep. I dared not linger. Getting up, I stretched, my hind end up high and my front legs before me. Much of my body hurt.

I was thirsty and hungry. Smoke still wisped in the distance. From what I could tell the second air ship was gone. No doubt the raiding Shadows had returned to the skies. I wondered how much longer the Lords would allow the raiders to do so before turning on them like a dog and ripping out their throats.

How I would like to be a part of that vengeance!

I turned in the opposite direction. As far as I could see nothing except black grayness. No blades of grass marred the surface. Broken burnt trees jutted out of cracks. The sun's heat made the surface hot and I hurried over it, hoping to find some place to cool my paws.

My tongue hung out of my mouth. It was so hot! My feet hurt. My body ached. A deep part of me began to long for death.

Suddenly my body slammed against the hot rock. I tried to rise. I couldn't. Heat pierced every part of me. I closed my eyes. Death at last had found me.I had a sense of movement. Something had me by the neck. Perhaps predators might roam this wasteland. I wanted to fight back. I had not the strength to do so.

How long I traveled thus I don't know. When next I awoke I heard the babbling of a stream and felt the coolness of grass beneath my body. I forced my eyes open. Not far away another feline lay, I could tell by the scent, but the size and fur I didn't know. It was white with black spots and far larger than me.

"You're awake." The large head turned to face me. Brown eyes stared into mine. I saw the very long tail draped over the greenery.

"Yes," I barely managed, wondering how I could understand the other.

"Mabon found you and brought you to me." The other licked its leg. "I am Kanya."

Female or so her musky odor betrayed her.

"You would have died. It is fortunate he was scouting for his pack."

Dogs traveled in packs. Did I owe my life to one? I found the idea revolting.

"We know the two legs came and killed each other." She got up and padded over to me. "Some left and went into the sky. Others on horses."

"You were watching."

"The pack sees much."

"Dogs," I spat.

"Wolves," she corrected. "Like me, they wander this land." I felt her nose against me. No doubt I was prey and would soon rest in her belly. "You will live." She went back to her spot and sat; her tail curled over her paws.

"Why am I here?" I struggled to stand. The water trickled over rocks. I wanted a drink. Warily I crossed the short distance and dared to lower my muzzle. The wetness felt good across my dry tongue and revived my tired, aching body.

"Long ago," she began. "We ran with your kind."

My head jerked up. My mother's stories!

"Many of us passed through the portal."

"But not all," I said.

"No. Not all." She turned her head toward me. "You now have a choice."

How?

When I made no reply, she went on. "It has long been said those who remained behind would not be forgotten. That Moon would return for us."

My mother hadn't told me that!

Kanya lifted her nose and sniffed. "The humans are beginning to return to this place. We must be gone."

She didn't need to explain. I understood the danger.

"There are a few who live here," she looked into the night. "They are cruel and hate us."

No doubt the banished. So. Some did survive despite the Lord's threats.

"Come." She trotted to the tree line.

I waited and then followed. Darkness engulfed us. I didn't

hear her passage. I kept her scent in my nose. When we left the forest, we stood on a high ledge. Below was a valley and in it, I couldn't believe what I saw, were hundreds of cats, canine creatures I assumed must be wolves and more like Kanya.

"We are gathering," she told me.

"What if the humans find us?"

"They have tried. This is a difficult place for them to reach." Kanya lifted her head, her nostrils flared. "The pack is sharing a kill."

I too, smelled the fresh blood. I also heard a sound behind me. I whirled and hissed.

Human faces peered at us through the trees. Some held pointed sticks. Others clenched rocks. With a wild howl they raced toward us.

"Get below!" Kanya leapt over me and growled.

I ran down a narrow steep path. "Humans!"

Wolves pushed past me. One of the cat females urged me to follow her. We hid in many tiny caves which pocked a huge tunnel.

Snarls, howls, yips and other sounds from above. Bodies fell and smashed on the hard rock. I dared to look. None of them were canine or feline.

When the battle ended, Kanya and the wolves returned to us. We shared the kill and I slept with a full belly.

Many sunrises came and went. Females attended my wound. My paws were not as damaged as I thought they'd be. Kanya chewed bark and licked the mixture on them. It eased what little pain I still felt. I began to heal.

I began to think of myself as safe, until the sky ship dropped down out of the sky upon us. The Shadows swarmed over the railing and I saw the evil smile of Lord Harrot. Had he planned for me to escape hoping I would lead him to others like me?

I wanted him dead. I wanted vengeance for the killing of my friend Captain Umbra and for the crew. Not to mention the deaths of so many cats I had no doubt he'd murdered.

"Wait," Kanya said, when I dared to creep forward in the defensive line. The females and their young were behind us. We'd been backed into the tunnel. Odd, the Shadows had not rushed us and began killing.

"Fire," Lord Harrot said. "They're trapped. Fire purifies."

A few Shadows guarded the entrance. I knew the damage fire

would do. Most of us would strangle before the flames consumed out bodies.

Stacks of wood began to be piled, along with dried grasses. The Lord stood there and grinned. I growled at him.

"Our kittens!" one of the females yowled.

I felt warmth behind me. I dared to turn my head. Three small moons hovered, their bright blue light bathing the dark tunnel walls. From between them walked a silver white female, her slim tail gently swaying from side to side.

"Come," she beckoned.

Several kittens hurried past her, pausing before plunging into the light. They vanished. Others followed. I turned my head back and growled a challenge. We needed to protect the females and their young.

Lord Harrot took what I knew to be a fire stick from his pocket. It lit and he tossed it on the grasses. They licked into flame, rapidly spreading.

"They can't see." The odd female stood beside me. "The portal is only for us."

"What of them?" I meant the great cats and wolves.

"They see it too." She licked my muzzle. "I am Moon. Come, Climber. Leave these two legs to their misguided future."

I followed Moon as did the other spotted cats, Kanya and lastly the wolves.

Pressure against my body, a sense of falling and then I stood upon a world like a cat could only dream of. I briefly wondered if I had passed beyond, but I did not see Bast's great temple.

"Welcome," Moon said. "To Bubastis."

Just like my mother's stories!

Lighthouses have a long history of being beacons warning sailors at night of bad weather or hazardous conditions. The buildings also are often occupied by lonely men or women and most have ghosts. Keeping the Tradition is a spin on that history of a ghost, a cat and lighthouse keeper in space.

Keeping the Tradition

Mable sighed with satisfaction as three times the lights flashed. The first was red, marking the Sheller quadrant in space. The second was blue indicating the Ramble system. The third designated the nearest planet Granite and was a pale gray.

"So dated," she mumbled as the light continued its pattern, her hands busy cleaning the thin metal on which the odd rainbow reflected. A slight cold passed by her, making her shiver. She dismissed it. Sometimes the heating wasn't even. She'd have to check the coils later and make sure they weren't losing power.

"Rerow."

The middle-aged woman smiled at her only companion, a long-haired Maine Coon with bright yellow eyes who she'd named Rumble. The large tom had the loudest purr she'd ever heard.

She knelt to rub a hand over his fur marveling how he didn't have the normal stripes most tabbies did. Instead he was a solid brown with a white bib on his chest.

"You're a very handsome cat," she complimented.

Rumble bumped against her leg leaving hair on her black pants. She smiled. No matter what she owned she was always properly furred and scented. It was her cat's way of marking her for his own.

"Hungry?"

In answer Rumble went to the spiraling steps down. He turned his head as if to say, 'Well, are you coming?'

Putting the cloth aside, she could always finish cleaning later, Mable followed her cat down into the main living area. It was larger than the quarters they'd shared when they'd been transported out to her lonely post. Lighthouse duty, whether on land or in space, was only for those who didn't mind spending endless hours alone.

She didn't mind as long as she had Rumble and other distractions besides the long hours of maintenance required to keep the light going. Passing ships depended on accurate locations so none got lost in the vast blackness of space. It was her job to keep the light going, just like those who had protected the Earth's shores centuries ago.

"Errrp." Rumble impatiently waited for his dinner. Mable shook her head and oozed a fishy smelling meal out into a bowl. Placing it on the metal floor she went to the communications console, which took up one dull white wall, to see if there were any important messages.

Not that she had any family to send her personal letters. Most who took these posts didn't since it was a lifetime assignment. Mable had worked many years in the space merchant service to get this post and was happy with her new duties.

There weren't any messages and that suited her just fine. Messages meant more to do than just maintaining her home, the computers, various electronics and the light.

"Now, what's for dinner?" She went to the other side of the room and rummaged through her various supplies. There was a small cooking unit, a huge pantry filled with containers, and another she kept a few keepsake dishes in.

Every year a ship came through and dropped off food, parts and anything else she might need. Oh, she might request a special shipment now and then, if she needed parts, but due to expense, it was better to get everything at once.

Besides, being disturbed more than once a year interrupted her blessed peace. After serving many years on merchant ships and sharing quarters with others, listening to hours of gossip, and having to be bossed around by the captain, not having any privacy had nearly driven her crazy.

Rumble finished his dinner and padded back up the spiral stairs. She figured he'd probably go take a nap on her bed. It was part of his normal routine and one she was comfortable with.

Choosing a can of tomato soup, she warmed it and sipped the hot contents while settling down on the puffy red chair, shoved under the stairs. She grabbed a book from the small bookcase next to it and read. Reading was one of her private pleasures and one she'd had to put aside while serving on the crowded ships.

Many peaceful hours passed. Mable finally pulled herself out of the world her book had plunged her into. She glanced up to find Rumble unsteadily on his hind legs, his front paws resting on the slight edge of the round window, gazing out at the twinkling stars.

"There's nothing out there." She stretched and put her soup container into the recycler.

Her cat turned his head and blinked his eyes, while his bushy tail swung back and forth.

"Or do you just like looking out?" She'd had a few cats growing up and knew most of them enjoyed windows. Her mother, now long dead, had always said it was a form of entertainment for them.

"Errr." He plopped down and jumped into her vacated chair. With his pink tongue he began grooming his shoulder.

"Like you didn't do that earlier," she teased. Rumble seemed to spend a lot of time grooming.

She yawned and realized she was tired. It was hard to tell how long she'd really been up. There was no night or day in space so humans just slept when they felt like it or on a forced schedule, as she'd had to do for years on those disagreeable ships.

"Night." Slowly Mable ascended the stairs, her boots making hollow clinks. On the next level was her small bedroom, with a nice thick blue comforter spread invitingly on her bed. She also had a tiny bathroom so she had to keep Rumble's litter box outside the door. There as a pungent smell escaping from it.

"Thanks a lot."

It didn't take long to clean it up. Once done she pulled off her black jumpsuit and tossed it aside. A quick brief shower and she settled down to sleep. She felt the familiar plunk indicating Rumble had joined her. His loud purr filled the room and she fell asleep to his comforting music.

Hissing and growling awoke Mable. She blinked her brown eyes several times, her slowly graying hair down in her face. She pushed it aside and looked around the room trying to figure out what made the cat so angry.

"There's nothing…" she began and shivered. The air was ice cold and she had the sense she was not alone. "Who's there?" she demanded.

Rumble was on the carpeted floor and hissing at a shimmering something pressed against the wall.

Mable muttered a few choice words as she pulled on a brown jumpsuit. Tucking her feet into her boots, she glared at the unwelcome intruder. Figured. The best post she'd had in her entire career and she was saddled with a ghost.

"You need to leave," she ordered.

The ghost pulsated a faint pink and slid along the wall. Rumble followed its every move, growling continually.

"I want to be alone. Go away." Mable marched into the restroom to tame her unruly hair and splash some water on her face. It helped her wake up.

Back in her bedroom she noted with disapproval the ghost had floated up the stairs to the light. Rumble was right behind, swiping at the nonexistent feet with his claws.

"Just great." Mable had heard stories of haunted light houses back on Earth and there were whispers of it out in space. Most space merchants didn't talk about such things. It was superstitious nonsense and many held the belief if you talked about one, it would haunt you.

Stomping up the stairs Mable watched the ghost as it hovered around the flashing light.

"You stay away from there," she warned. "It's needed to protect ships."

Rumble hissed, holding his ground. His tail swished constantly.

"And why did you show up now?" Mable frowned. "I've been here for nearly six months."

There was no answer and she didn't really expect one. Ghosts didn't talk.

Slowly her unwelcome guest faded and Rumble sniffed at the spot where the ghost had stood. Mable leaned down and saw faded blood stains on the deck.

"Hmmm." Rising, she thoughtfully looked at the stains. Had one of the previous keepers fallen and without help perished? Or had one of them died under mysterious and unsolved circumstances?

"Looks like we have mystery to solve," she told Rumble. "I don't know about you, but I always think better after breakfast."

~ * ~

A veggie omelet filled her stomach and she fed Rumble chicken. Retreating once more to the chair, she held the written keepers log on her lap. Rumble jumped up to join her, draping his massive bulk half on her upper leg.

"It's not convenient to have you sitting there." Not that the cat would pay any attention to her.

He put his paw on the log and she gently pushed it away. "No." Carefully she turned the pages. Most everyone else used the computer to keep logs, personal journals and make reports. Light keepers kept the written tradition.

A large part of the log information were mundane recordings of supply ships arriving, what they'd received, astronomical observations, daily records of maintenance, sometimes the name of passenger liners as they went by. But one, dating back a hundred years, was entirely different.

I hate it here. I've requested to be reassigned but it's been denied several times. I'm going mad. There's nothing out here. I'm so lonely!

"Then you shouldn't have asked to be assigned here." Mable kept turning pages. More facts and figures, then:

Last supply ship had a litter of kittens. One of the crewmen took pity on me and gave me a cat. She's really cute. Karlin, that's what I decided to name her, has short white fur and the brightest golden eyes I've ever seen.

She's not more than two months old. I was told she's a great mouser. Guess that will come in handy in the event one of my supply shipments has some unwelcome guests.

Mable pet Rumble's head. He'd killed more than a few mice and a rat or two, in the shipments she'd gotten. Her cat spent time down in the hold area. Not every day, but enough to make her think she had some pests.

"At least the keeper got a cat." Cats were a long time tradition.

Karlin is the sweetest thing and sleeps with me at 'night'.

"Just like you do."

Rumble answered with a loud purr. His eyes were half closed in pleasure.

More facts, observations, but not much else so Mable sighed and closed the log.

"I really don't like mysteries and I certainly don't like having a ghost around."

But, there might be more tidbits someplace if she could just figure out where to look. Mable pushed Rumble off her lap. He glared at her and jumped down, disappearing down the stairs.

"Have fun mouse hunting." Mable went back up to the light, spending the day polishing the metal and making adjustments. She tried not to look at the faded blood patch on the floor. Whatever had happened here didn't really concern her. She just wanted her private time.

Again a chill filled the room. Mable groaned. "Oh, go away, will ya? I've got work to do."

After several long minutes the cold faded away. "Thanks."

Obviously the ghost was going to be a nuisance and she needed to get rid of it. The only way to do that was to figure out why whoever it was haunted the light.

After another dinner of soup, vegetable beef this time and a grilled cheese sandwich, Mable broke into her chocolate chip cookies and had a glass of milk. Munching on the sweet treat, she plopped the keeper log on her lap. There just had to be more records.

Similar writing she'd seen before caught her eye.

I can't find Karlin anywhere. I've searched every nook and cranny. There's just nowhere for her to hide.

"Urrp."

Mable glanced down at Rumble. He was looking up at her. "What?"

He went to the stairs and looked down, then back at her.

"Am I supposed to follow you?"

"Rerow."

"That a yes?" Mable put the log aside and got up. Immediately Rumble began descending. "Guess so."

She followed her cat. The lights sprang on. They stayed off to conserve power. Rumble didn't trip them on his numerous trips below. He was too small.

"Rumble?" Problem with cats is they never came when you called.

A loud yowl reached her ears. Mable weaved among the boxes, trying to figure out where the cat was. She found him on the far side, his nose pushing against something white.

"What have you found?" She reached out and realized it was fur. "Oh, no." With trembling fingers she gently worked between the boxes and the wall.

"Huh?" Something didn't feel right. Instead of a decayed body, she pulled out a live tiny cat. Two golden eyes blinked at her and a mournful meow escaped from its mouth.

"This is just not possible." She put the cat next to Rumble who immediately began bathing it. Mable got down on her hands and knees, peering into the odd corner. Flashing jagged lines spiraled out, retracted, seemed to go backwards before repeating the cycle.

"Great, an energy spider." They weren't common but they did, from time to time invade ships or light houses. No one really knew where they came from and they were very difficult to get rid of.

She didn't want to lose Rumble so she searched through her supplies, trying to find something to trap it and keep her cat from getting trapped. In a small box she found some emergency webbing, normally only kept on ships, and used the tacky ends to secure it on the metal walls.

"That ought to hold you."

The creature expanded and contracted. She heard an odd crackle as if the spider was angry.

She stuck out her tongue. "Serves you right." Mable gathered up both cats and took them back upstairs. Putting them on the floor, she closed the hatch. If there were any mice down there, the spider could have them.

She fed Rumble some turkey and gently urged the white cat to take a few bites. It didn't seem to be too hungry. She checked the cat's sex and knew it was a female.

"I wonder." Energy spiders were notorious for keeping their prey alive for a long, long time. Since they weren't studied, there was no way to know for how many years their captives could live.

"I'll bet you're Karlin."

The cat blinked. Rumble began grooming the female and she heard a faint purr from Karlin.

Determined now to figure out what had happened, Mable picked up the log and flipped forward several pages.

I've looked for days and can't find her. I have no idea what happened. I really miss her.

Days later there was another entry.

I can't stand being alone and they're continually refusing to reassign me. Now, I'm hearing haunting meows and I just can't stand it.

The room got ice cold. Mable jerked up. The ghost was getting very annoying.

Rumble hissed, his brown hair spiking along his back. Karlin rose shakily to her and mewed.

The white shimmering seemed to bend down as if to stroke the white cat.

"Yes," Mable heard herself saying. "I found your cat."

Like the flying ghosts she'd seen on cartoons during her childhood, the pulsating ripple whirled and zipped through a crack to the lower level. Mable found herself on her feet following. She made sure to close the hatch. No way was she going to lose her two companions.

In the far corner the flashing spider was clawing at the webbing she'd put up. The ghost had turned a bright red, rolling itself into a tight ball.

Not sure what was going to happen, Mable watched as her ghost smashed through the webbing. The lightening tendrils embraced the red ball and there was a thunderous clap. Bright white flashed out and she cried out, covering her eyes.

When she could see again, a scorch mark was burned into the wall. All evidence of the trap and the energy spider was gone.

"Whew!" It seemed the threat, however long it had been there, was gone. So was her ghost. "Thanks," she said to the previous keeper.

~ * ~

Six months later her supply ship arrived. The captain greeted her warmly although he frowned at the sight of her two cats.

"Thought you had only one."

Mable smiled. "Long story."

"I see." His eyes narrowed. "There was a keeper once who had a white cat."

"Saw that entry. It dated back a hundred years."

He nodded. "I'm surprised they didn't tell you this light was haunted by a keeper who took her own life."

"Not anymore."

"What?"

Mable laughed. She watched both cats scamper through the new boxes. "Why don't you join me for dinner, Captain. It's an interesting tale."

Darkness in the Heartland presents angels in an unique way, one which caught the editor by surprise who wasn't looking for them to be animals. The story was accepted and even mentioned in the introduction. What was not shared is that the place and event were real, with some changes, but the eventual outcome similar.

Darkness in the Heartland

His paws hit the concrete slabs surrounding the fountain. Lifting his massive head he sniffed the night breeze. The smell of humans, mixed with their food, flowers, trees and other scents, including a timid rabbit nearby, tickled his nose. He wasn't there to hunt the rightful prey. His assignment was far different and much more important.

He lowered his mouth to take a sip of water. It was cold and quenched his thirst. When he was finished he used his tongue to clean his shoulder. It was difficult to go much further than that. His huge wings made grooming that annoying spot behind his neck almost impossible. He had to depend on others of his kind, the few who had been created, to do it for him.

Several thuds sounded nearby. He stopped grooming and blinked his yellow-brown eyes. Shapes materialized out of the darkness. They were all orange with black stripes, their furred wings blending into their hide perfectly.

Not that he would have expected it to be any different. It was the way the Creator had made them.

Circe jumped up on the slab, rising on her hind legs, placing her front paws on the pedestal. What appeared to be an open book rested there. It had writing etched into the copper pages. She chuffed, dropping down and padded over to him.

"It's too bad their leader did not truly read the book," she said. "If he had, then we would not have to be here."

"True," he agreed. "But we are and must do what we sent to do."

"Gabron," she addressed him by his name. Her green eyes darted to the three others who joined them. "It has been long since we've been asked to do such."

"Too long." He gazed upon the three others, knowing each well. Limpet, who had battled the ultimate Dark One in a battle he had only heard stories of. Moutia, proud and lovely, having the honor of being present at the birth of the Son, and Ginger, newest of their number and yet to prove herself.

"We all know why we're here," Gabron said.

The others sat on their haunches. Their wings folded upon their backs. He didn't need to repeat their instructions. Gabron knew that, but he spoke anyway.

"The first leader of this group has died. He left behind a proud, haughty pretender who takes advantage of women," he said as the females growled. "He increases prejudice against any who will not blindly follow him and pretends to follow the Most High when instead, he serves the purpose of the Dark One" He opened his mouth, his huge canines glistening in the faint moon light. "He is destroying the lives of thousands of humans." Limpet hissed. "Our job is *not* to kill him but stop the theatrical production before it is presented. It will be in the main event tent."

"Seems a silly thing," Ginger said, her head tilted as if she were puzzled.

"This production will do much damage. The leader of this group has cast himself as the hero and woman, who he sleeps with daily, as the villain."

"And, they are not mated," Moutia said. "Such is not the will of the Creator. He has given this one a wonderful wife and child."

"So." Ginger lifted her paw and pulled at a claw with her teeth. "He does not appreciate what he has."

"No." Gabron sniffed the breeze again. "Soon, they will drift to their tents to sleep. Only a few will be awake to watch." A branch broke nearby. "A human comes. We must hide." Already in his mind the image of small gully behind them, where they would not be seen. Over it was a wooden bridge.

The five drifted to the hiding spot, bedding down in the tall, sweet grasses as the creek gurgled nearby. Sometimes, he heard laughing and humans speaking together.

When the moon began to drop, silence reigned.

"It is time," he told the others. He rose and they left the hiding place. Walking once again past the beautiful fountain, Gabron found it unfortunate such a smothering darkness had sprang up in the heartland. Nearby cows mooed at each other and the wind rustled through the fields, now tall with crops that soon would be harvested.

He avoided the road. There were sentries there, not to mention those who stalked it to try and retrieve a lost loved one and bring them home. Instead, the winged warriors silently passed through the trees, into the huge parking lot. Gabron glanced at the plates, surprised there were so many from the various states.

A lone human sat in an open tent, humming to itself. It didn't see them.

Once they had reached the camping area, he paused. Getting through the maze to where they needed to go would be tricky. They could not wake any human. Not that any would believe what they saw and even if they did, they might think them demons instead of the Creator's messengers.

"This way," he instructed, leading the way past tents of various sizes and shapes. He paused now and again as someone roused, making sure they did not wake, before leading the others onward.

Eventually, they came to the main area. Huge tents were set up everywhere. Some were for cooking and serving foods. Others were for the 'classes' that were taught every day. Further on were buildings that housed the staff and the products that were sold during this meeting. In the center sat a huge tent, the top a striped green and white.

"That is where we must go." He padded forward, using his nose to push aside the light flap.

Inside were rows and rows of chairs of non-padded chairs and hard metal bleachers lined the sides. In the center was a huge wooden stage. Upon it were stairs with poles and towers that looked sort of like ladders. There seemed to be a pit and he could detect the scent of propane.

"Come." He trotted down the aisle, intent on beginning the needed destruction. He stopped, sensing something not right.

"Out demons!" A brown-haired man appeared on the stage. The tight-fitting costume did little to hide his 'assets' and showed off the trim, muscular figure. "This is God's place."

God's place? Gabron knew better. He gazed upon the human and saw the pure black evil consuming the human's blue eyes.

With a snarl he launched himself, landing easily upon the

wood. He lashed out his huge paw at the human, who danced back and released a curdling laugh.

"You can't stop what is going to happen here!"

The others were circling around, each taking a corner, as if to protect Gabron from any type of attack. Circe knocked over a tower and rent it with her claws. Ginger pounced upon another, knocking it over, while Limpet shredded it. Moutia worked on the pit, pulling out the odd spouts with her teeth.

"Stop!" the human shouted. "Stop in the name of…"

Moutia hissed, stopping the other from speaking the powerful name. It would have no effect on them, but it would blasphemy coming from the human who did not serve the True One.

Roaring, the human grabbed one of the broken metal rungs. Madly swinging the weapon it advanced upon Gabron.

"I'll show you!"

Instinct took over and Gabron swiped at the human's leg. Deep, bleeding rents cut tendon and muscle, yet still, the enraged creature advanced upon him.

Limpet leaped to his defense, snarling, teeth bared.

"No," Gabron ordered. "This battle is mine."

"He serves the Dark One."

"It is my battle. Finish what we came here to do."

Reluctantly the oldest of them continued the destruction, while Gabron circled the evil leader. It still swung its weapon, trying to knock him unconscious. Not that it would work. It would have if he were just a tiger, but he wasn't.

Things were moving in the shadows and he knew a moment of fear. The other dancers in the production were advancing, shuffling, as if held enthralled. Their eyes were glassy. They held wooden branches, knives, even a few guns. Guns that the leader denied, passionately, they even had, the few times the authorities had come to check out the rumors.

There was more movement outside and he saw the shadows of the other followers reflected upon the tent sides. They moaned as if they were banshees, their fingers clawing at the fabric, trying to tear it apart to get to inside.

Gabron released a full battle roar and leapt upon the leader. He knocked the human down, trying to grasp the frail throat in his jaws. Inhuman strong hands grasped his in return, trying to choke the life from him.

They toppled end over end, knocking down clanking objects, until they rested upon one of the pits. The human wildly reached for something. Gabron saw the control and sank his fangs into the soft flesh.

The leader screamed, his black eyes smoking a fury not born of the human world. It was echoed by the dancers and followers who rushed forward trying to stop both the fight and the task he and the others had been sent to stop.

"To the air!" He ordered his companions. Luckily the tent was high, like those of the circuses. His ears heard the sharp snap and swoosh of wings as they obeyed.

"UnGodly monster!" the human yelled, still trying to choke Gabron.

"Follower of Darkness," he replied. "Do you not think the Creator has looked down and seen what you have corrupted?"

"Unholy demon!"

"Adulterer."

"Vile devil!"

"Teacher of untruth."

"Kill it!" he shouted to the hypnotized dancers and followers.

"Stop!" Gabron's order echoed through the tent and out into the night. The humans hesitated, some shaking their heads, others looking around as if wondering how they got there.

Trying once again, the leader's fingers grasped the control. White fire whirled up, engulfing their forms. Gabron sat, ideally washing blood from his paw.

Laughing in triumphant the leader got to his feet, his outfit smoldering.

Gabron stopped grooming and blinked his eyes. "You forget human, I can not be burned."

"Just proves you're a demon!"

Smoke was beginning to fill the tent. The fire snaked along its path, catching anything that would burn. The other humans were mumbling as if unsure what to do.

"Get them out!" he ordered the others.

He watched his companions fly down, herding the humans out, many of whom shrieked in terror.

"I am not to kill you," Gabron told the leader.

The leader began to laugh, raising his arms, as the flames licked at his body. "I can't be killed! I'm the Chosen One! The rightful successor. I was picked to lead this group! They'll obey me!"

Confused cries came from outside. Distantly Gabron herd the wail of a fire engine.

"You need to leave or you'll die."

"No!" The human ran to the leaning tower and began to climb it. "I'll will triumphant!"

What am I to do? he asked the Creator of all Things.

The choice has been made. Leave him to his fate.

The winged tiger bounded away from the fire. He rejoined the rest of the winged warriors who were perched on the distant roof. Blue and orange flames whirled into the air, the tent flapping like a distressed bird with a broken wing. Fireman shouted to each other, water gushing from the hoses as they attempted to stop the spread.

One spark streaked across, landing on the neighboring tent. It too erupted, spreading the danger even further.

The followers panicked, running from the main area, back toward the safety of the camp.

All through the night Gabron watched as the cleansing fire eradicated the meeting area, even managing to take several buildings with it. With the moist dawn, the ground was black and ruined, faint whisps of smoke sometimes twirling.

"He's dead!" someone screamed.

The few who had not eventually fled in their cars, abandoning their tents, and fleeing to freedom, slowly gathered near.

"The dance presentation was to have been our victory over the Devil!" A woman knelt next to the blackened corpse. Tears were on her cheeks. Gabron suspected it was the leader's wife. "We must bury him. He deserves that much."

Gently they reverently gathered the charred smelling remains on a sheet. They slowly walked away, carrying the fabric as if it were a coffin. In many ways, Gabron reflected, it was.

"Our job is done," Gabron told them.

"Yes," Circe agreed.

The other three spread their striped wings and flew away into the clear blue day.

Circe rubbed against his side. "You did not kill him."

"No. He chose death for himself."

"They have that choice."

"I know." He licked her muzzle. "Thank you."

"As always." She leaped into the sky, circling the compound once, before flying through the windows into heaven.

He sat there for a few more hours observing the outcome. The very few remaining loyal began to clean up the mess. But, he sensed the damage had been done. The cult would never again be as powerful as it once had been.

Maybe that in truth had been their true assignment. The Creator did not always tell them everything.

With that final comforting revelation, Gabron launched into the sky.

Author's Bio

Dana Bell enjoys writing regional Colorado tales and has lived in various other places, which serve as settings for her stories. Some star the many cats she's been owned by. Her works include her novels *Winter Awakening* and *God's Gift,* a cat vampire short story series, and various odd tales. She has edited several anthologies including *Different Dragons, Different Dragons 2, Supernatural Colorado, Love 'em, Shoot 'em* and *Extinct?* For fun, Dana builds and decorates doll houses and colors in her coloring books. Her paranormal short story and novella romances are under her pen name Belle Blukat.

More Cat Adventures

If you enjoyed this collection and would like to read more cat adventures, the following short story titles are available in the following anthologies.

Creeping Cold another lighthouse tale in The Young Explorer's Adventure Guide.

The following are available in the Planetary Anthology series. *First Cat in Space* a spin on a crashing spaceship above Venus. *Abandoned Children* told by a sand cat living on Mars. *Doing My Job* mixes my cat vampires, post Winter Trilogy and the Five Systems/Borders universe heading for Saturn.

Will of the Goddess a Chosen One visits a quaint English village. Published in Whitstead Christmastide: A Speculative Anthology.

Other WolfSinger Books
By Dana Bell

Winter Awakening

Terrified shrieks reached Word Warrior's ears as he floundered up the embankment. In the gully below he saw the blood-stained snow and the dead corpse of the screaming kitten's mother. A stinky shaggy two-leg was trying to capture the youngster and he knew it couldn't be allowed to. With a battle cry born of his ancestors he charged down the hill—unaware of the high hunter lurking in the pines.

In the storm filled mountains, Anumati heard scratching at the entrance of her den. Her every instinct was to protect the three young who lay at her side. Her body tensed for battle as two howlers padded in.

World Warrior and Anumati are unaware kittens, pups and rightful prey are being stolen by strange metal monster. All that is left behind are odd jagged paw prints of an animal they do not know.

In their world of snow and biting wind they must decide if they trust each other enough to find out the truth or if old predator-prey rules remain with no hope for change.

God's Gift

Major Larry Henry had never expected to hear those words spoken by an alien race. Let alone one with sharp claws and fangs they used for hunting and could easily shred him, his youngest sister and her boyfriend to shreds! But when his other sister Susanna and their good friend Kal Devon disappeared from their colony, Larry and the rescue party made the astonishing discovery they weren't alone on Galilahi.

Yet Kal had hinted there were secrets being kept from the colonists. Both his friend's sister and Susanna's husband had been killed in hover accidents. The civilian and military leaders made a show of agreeing in public while Larry knew about the conflicts between them. Susanna had made discoveries about the dark fates of earlier colonies. Not to mention a jump in technology which should have taken centuries of evolution not just a few decades.

Now stranded on Galilahi with no way to relocate or return to Earth, Larry found himself wondering if the human colonists could co-exist with the feline natives or if human history would repeat itself.

Or did the God Larry believed in and trusted, have another plan none of them knew about?

Extinct? – edited by Dana Bell

What if those ancient creatures so beloved in fiction, myth, and science had not disappeared? What if they were real? What might have been developed to handle them, and how might man have felt about the thundering giants in yesterday's, today's, or tomorrow's worlds.

Imagine a sanctuary established for dinosaurs that displaces humans.

What if Raptors were used on a distance planet as scouts for the new colony?

Could Dodo birds have left a record about what happened to them? Dragons helping settlers? Inconceivable!

A conqueror learns a hard lesson from a goddess and two children create their own 'monster'.

Lovely, unique, tales of lumbering giants of old, ancient rulers of the skies, and many others once thought to be myth or legend appear here in Extinct?

Cat Tails – edited by Dana Bell and Rebecca McFarland Kyle

Cats have been our companions since long before they graced the temples of Ancient Egypt. In addition to being members of our families, they have also stood with us through difficult times. From keeping pests and vermin away from our food stores to providing a comforting paw when we have been wounded; cats have been our sidekicks and friends in many different battles.

Learn more at www.wolfsingerpubs.com.

Made in the USA
Las Vegas, NV
07 February 2023

67035299R00079